Loa
re
Li
wi

P

HAWKER'S BIG PUSH

By the same author:

Hawker's War, The Book Guild, 1998

HAWKER'S BIG PUSH

John Hogston

The Book Guild Ltd
Sussex, England

First published in Great Britain in 2003 by
The Book Guild Ltd
25 High Street
Lewes, East Sussex
BN7 2LU

Typesetting in Baskerville by
SetSystems Ltd, Saffron Walden, Essex

Printed in Great Britain by
Bookcraft (Bath) Ltd, Avon

A catalogue record for this book is
available from the British Library

ISBN 1 85776 720 9

ACKNOWLEDGEMENTS

Part Two of this story was written with close reference to Trevor Pidgeon's wonderful book: *The Tanks at Flers*. Even so, my account of 15 September 1916 is necessarily incomplete and is particularly unfair to the men of 'C' Company, Heavy Section, Machine Gun Corps, who also took the field on that day. Those requiring a full and true account of the tank's debut in battle should read *The Tanks at Flers*. It is a masterpiece of gripping narrative, crucial fact and stunning detail and fitting tribute to the tank men of 1916/18 whose courage and dogged application to their new trade broke the bloody mould of trench warfare and made Allied victory possible.

I am grateful to Giles Allen and Arthur Cole, for their knowledge, advice and constant support; and to Roy Cox, the magician who gave me the card trick and the idea.

Thanks are also due to Spinning Top Limited, Swindon, who provided the maps.

PROLOGUE – AUGUST 1914

'Cavalry!'

The sentry's cry was edged with panic and cracked with thirst and fatigue.

Sergeant Garrett, lying with the remains of his platoon in the meagre shade beside the sunken road, looked up as if he had been kicked.

'God Almighty,' he muttered under his breath, 'that's all we need!'

There came the rattle of the sentry's rifle-bolt and Garrett shouted urgently, 'Don't fire, I'm coming up!'

His thigh muscles screamed at him but he forced himself up the steep bank and bellowed over his shoulder at his men, 'Move yourselves, there's cavalry sighted!'

He threw himself full length beside the sentry.

'Take it easy, Tyke. Where are they?'

The sentry pointed excitedly.

'There, Sarge. They're charging straight at us.'

The sergeant held one hand up against the glare of the late morning sun while he fished the captain's binoculars out of their leather case.

'What are they?' he asked. 'Can you see any lances? Uhlans carry lances.'

'They're too far away to see, Sarge, but they're not French. Frog cavalry wear brass helmets and breastplates. You can see them shining miles away.'

1

Garrett gave the boy a surprised glance. Tyke was inclined to be exciteable but was a good lad. He was as done in as his mates but had kept a sharp lookout. He'd make a good soldier if he got time. He had the binoculars out now and focused them carefully on the approaching body of horsemen. After a moment he grunted with relief. The flat caps and khaki uniforms were clearly visible.

'It's all right,' he told the sentry. 'They're ours. Only five of 'em.'

'Maybe they can let us have some water, Sarge,' the sentry said hopefully.

'Don't bet on it,' Garrett replied bitterly. 'If they've got water, they'll save it all for the bloody horses.'

His feeling of relief was fast turning to one of regret. In their present state, he would rather his men didn't have to suffer the scrutiny of British cavalry.

The sergeant looked distastefully over his shoulder. Between the high banks of the sunken road there flowed a teeming flood of humanity. An endless stream of refugees were pouring from the broken towns of Namur, Charleroi and Mons and fleeing frantically south. The roads were clogged with a motley assortment of transport: wagons pulled by oxen; farm carts drawn by heavy horses; carts tugged by ponies, donkeys and dogs. And people: packed masses pushing hastily gathered possessions on bicycles, tricycles, prams and barrows; women and old men with bundles in their arms and on their backs; children clutching toys and pets. All surging southwards, to Paris and safety.

Hindered and jostled by this torrent of misery were the struggling remnants of an army. On the outbreak of war, the British Expeditionary Force: eighty thousand men under Sir John French, had been rushed across the Channel and force-marched eastwards to stand beside their French allies. They had encountered the German army at Mons and stopped the grey tide in its tracks. But as the hard-pressed French fell back on Paris, the British too were ordered to give ground, being wide open to an attack on their unguarded flank. It was full-scale retreat. Orderly and unpanicked, but retreat. To the soldiers, unbeaten in battle, it was inexplicable. And so they marched: angrily and bitterly, and ever more desperate. Apart from a few hours snatched at night, they had been marching non-stop for five days. Five sweltering days in the baking sun, with little water and no food.

The sergeant looked at his men. Barely a dozen were left of a whole platoon. None of them had moved at the sentry's warning and several were fast asleep. The ragged band were an orderly officer's nightmare. All had beards. Many had cut their tunic sleeves off at the elbow. Few wore puttees, so that their bare legs showed startlingly white between ruined boots and knickerbocker breeches which ended, unfastened, below the knees. Many had knotted handkerchiefs on their heads and those that still had caps wore them reversed to protect their necks from the worst of the sun. During a previous halt, some had foolishly removed their boots, only to find that their feet had swollen to twice normal size. To get their boots back on, they had to slit the backs with a bayonet and tie them on their feet with puttees. Socks had worn through in the first days of forced-march and blisters had risen and burst so that, as the men marched, their boots slopped disgustingly with sweat, pus and blood.

As the horsemen came closer, Garrett saw from their badges that they were Scots Greys. At first this puzzled him, then he looked carefully at the horses and saw that they had been painted with iodine to make them less conspicuous. It was evident that they had been in fight. The group stank of cordite and while one man wrapped a rudimentary bandage around a slashed forearm, the others reloaded their pistols. Animals and men sweated profusely but they were not fatigued. Rather their exertions had brought them to a fine edge; men and beasts shone with health. There was no overt display of arrogance. In fact the troopers hardly acknowledged the ragged infantrymen who had once worn the same uniform as themselves. But there was a pride about them, and a purpose, and even the horses seemed to harbour a pitying disdain for all lesser forms of life who were not cavalry; not Scots Greys.

The detachment was led by a captain – an exaggerated rank, the sergeant thought, for so small a force. A young captain, in his late twenties, but exuding confidence and command. A big man, taller in the saddle than his companions, with unfashionably long hair and a fair, clipped moustache. The well-chiselled, aristocratic face had been deep-bronzed by a sun more brutal than that of northern France. An Empire man, Garret guessed, or a fighting colonial who had returned to the motherland at the first signs of war.

The captain reined in his mount beside Garrett and his steel-blue eyes took in the moving column of refugees and the soldiers conspicuously inert beside the road.

The sergeant saluted vigorously.

'Sergeant Garrett, sir, King's Own. With eleven men heading for St Quentin.'

It was a beautiful salute, honed to perfection over 15 years' service and the officer acknowledged it generously, but his frown of disapproval remained.

'Captain Lovell, Scots Greys,' he said distantly. 'With respect, Sergeant, you're heading nowhere at present. Most of your men are asleep in the ditch.'

'Just a five-minute break, sir. The men are all in. We've been continually on the move for five days.' The sergeant hurried to capitalise on this. 'Sir, you wouldn't have any water to spare, by any chance? We ran out miles back.'

The officer shook his head.

4

'Not a drop, I'm afraid. We have to look after the horses.'

Behind him the troopers had dismounted and were wetting handkerchiefs with their water bottles and rubbing them over the horses' noses. Garrett heard the sentry's snort of amusement.

Several of the soldiers who had been lying at the roadside had now roused themselves and climbed the bank, joining the group of men and horses. Garrett felt unreasonable shame at their ramshackle appearance.

The captain looked at the newcomers with distaste, then turned again to their sergeant.

'Where are your officers?' he demanded.

One of the soldiers guffawed loudly. Garrett ignored him.

'Captain Bartholomew is dead, sir,' he replied. 'We lost him after Mons.'

The newcomer guffawed again.

'Pity it wasn't before Mons,' he retorted. He took a pace towards the mounted officer and addressed him insolently. 'Captain Bartholomew,' he said heavily, 'lost two thirds of us in a pointless bloody bayonet charge, then blew his own brains out when his horse was killed and he had to do a bit of hard marching. Left us to fend for ourselves, he did.'

'Shut up, Rogan!' Garrett said viciously.

The soldier had spoken the truth but he wouldn't have it discussed in front of strangers. Bartholomew had been a good peacetime officer but he was too old and unfit for active service. Totally exhausted after two days of forced march and half-crazed by the pain in his feet, he had hobbled into a cornfield and shot himself in the head.

But Private Rogan hadn't finished. He took another step towards the cavalry captain and held his rifle across his chest belligerently.

'And we don't need no advice from any bloody cavalry. Sling your hooks. Go on, piss off out of it!'

Captain Lovell's gaze changed from disdain to contempt. He still sat his horse calmly but his right hand, that had been resting easily on his thigh, now shifted to the buckle on his Sam Browne belt. Close to the buckle, was the butt of his pistol. The pistol was unusual in that it was carried reversed, to the left, in an open holster. All officers had pistols, but they were mostly worn as uniform accessories in closed holsters. Lovell's was carried in easy reach, as if he meant to use it.

Garrett acted quickly. He stepped forward.

'I said shut up, Rogan. Fall out!' He grabbed the soldier by his belt and shoved him away, then drew himself up and addressed the officer with dignity. 'I'm very sorry about that, sir. Private Rogan meant no direspect. He's a good soldier but a little overwrought. I'll make sure he's punished.'

Behind his back, Ryan continued to rave.

'Look at you,' he yelled contemptuously. 'You and you're bloody horses. What use are you?'

The captain continued to watch him closely. He addressed Garrett again.

'Are you sure you can handle that man, sergeant? He might have an unsettling effect on the rest of your men. I'll deal with him if you wish.'

Garrett smiled. Still looking the captain in the face he called behind him to the sentry.

'Private Tyke, is Private Rogan having an unsettling effect on you?'

'Not at all, Sergeant,' Tyke replied dutifully.

The sergeant nodded in satisfaction. 'That's because he's a brainless, ill-mannered pillock, isn't it, Tyke? What is he, Tyke?'

'He's a brainless, ill-mannered pillock, Sergeant,' Tyke intoned.

Still smiling, Garrett addressed the officer again.

'Thank you, sir, but I can handle it. I think we should be getting along now, sir.'

'Very well.'

Lovell seemed disappointed but his hand rested on his thigh again. He made to turn his horse away, then hesitated. He untied a water-bottle from the pommel of his saddle and removed another that hung from his shoulder. He leaned forward and held them out.

'I think we can spare these.'

Garrett took them gratefully.

'Thank you very much, sir.'

Lovell nodded.

'You're welcome. Just keep going. You should be all right. General Smith-Dorrien has checked the *Boche* at Le Cateau.'

He wheeled his horse and urged it into a canter, his troopers falling in behind.

'Good riddance to bad rubbish!' Rogan crowed. 'Look at him. Thinks he's back in India chasing the natives. Piss off out of it, Mad Dog bloody Lovell!'

He waved two fingers vehemently at the sky and slunk back down the bank.

The sergeant looked at Private Tyke and chuckled. He shook his head in astonishment.

'That bloody Rogan. What did he say? What did he call that officer?'

'Mad Dog Lovell,' the sentry said brightly. 'He's right, Sarge. That was Mad Dog Lovell. Didn't you recognise him?'

'Recognise him? I've never even heard of him!' Garrett said emphatically.

'Oh come on, Sarge,' the sentry said impatiently. 'you must remember. When we were moving up to Mons the Greys were billeted in the same farm as us. Their horses had better billets than we did. In the evening some of us went into the village to try and get a drink and fell in with

7

some of the Greys. They told us about old Lovell. He's Lord Lovell really. His old man is the Earl of something or other. He was in India before the war started. Did you see his Khyber Knife?'

'His what?' the sergeant asked incredulously.

'That bloody great knife he had on his belt. He chops off people's heads with it. He's a crack shot with a pistol, too. You should have let him take care of old Rogan. Then we'd have seen some fun!'

Garrett shook his head hopelessly.

'I've never heard a bigger load of rubbish in my life! I'm disappointed in you, Tyke. I had it in mind to put you up for a stripe, but now I think it was a mistake. You'll never make an NCO. You've got too much imagination.'

Tyke laughed ironically.

'I reckon you're right there, Sarge.' He shaded his eyes with his hand and squinted at the fast-diminishing group of men and horses. 'But Captain Lovell is a hell of a good soldier. He's lucky too. You're all right when you're with him. Look at them go,' he added wistfully. 'I wish I'd joined the cavalry.'

Captain Lovell's luck deserted him early the next day. They had spent the five hours of darkness in one of the many small copses that littered the landscape and were off again at first light, cantering just below the skyline. The shells hit them without warning in a bewildering rush of shocks and bangs that gave no time for coherent thought. Two troopers and their mounts were killed instantly. A third man was unhorsed by the blast and watched his terrified mount disappear into the distance. A fourth man had wheeled to pick up his stranded mate when another salvo fell, felling horse and rider and killing the man on foot.

The shelling ceased as suddenly as it had begun. Captain

Lovell who had galloped to the shelter of the reverse slope, cantered up surveying the shambles. Three men and two horses lay broken and still. The trooper who had turned back was weeping quietly beside his stricken horse. The animal's forelegs were smashed and it jerked its head in an effort to rise.

Lovell checked his horse and held out a hand.

'Come on, man,' he shouted. 'Up behind me!'

The boy turned up a miserable, tear-stained face.

'I can't leave her, sir,' he said plantively.

Lovell wheeled his mount and his pistol appeared in his hand.

'Get up behind me *now*,' he ordered. 'You know the importance of our mission. I can't leave a man behind to talk to the Huns.

'I can't, sir', the boy pleaded. 'I can't leave Bessie like this.'

Lovell cocked his pistol. He looked anxiously down the hill to where he deduced the firing to have come from, then turned again to his problem.

'Hold her then,' he said. 'Kneel on her neck.'

The trooper obeyed, still snivelling quietly. Lovell stilled his horse and took careful aim. The pistol cracked and the mare died instantly and without pain.

'Come on!' Lovell said urgently. The trooper stood up and limped towards him. Lovell stared in consternation. 'What's wrong with your leg?' he demanded.

'I twisted it when we fell, sir,' the boy replied absently. 'I don't think it's broken.'

He prepared to mount. Then he looked up into the officer's face – and froze. Lovell was looking at him coldly. The pistol was still in his hand; the hammer laid back.

'I can ride, sir!' the trooper said desperately.

A moment passed and Lovell grinned suddenly.

'Let's hope you can,' he said.

9

He extended his hand and the boy swung up behind.

They crossed to the far side of the ridge and cantered easily, heading west. After a while the trooper spoke again.

'Those shells, sir. They came from the south didn't they? Could the Huns have got ahead of us?'

'It's possible,' Lovell said over his shoulder. 'I'm going to head due west and hope for the best.'

Privately, he considered it more likely that the shells came from a jumpy French battery on the outskirts of Peronne, but he kept these thoughts to himself. He laid a hand on the two leather saddlebags slung each side of his horse's withers. It was quite possible that the Germans *had* swung a wide right hook towards Paris and this worried him. If there were Huns between himself and the Channel, the situation was serious. Two men on one horse couldn't ride out of trouble and even on his own it would be very risky. He wasn't worried about his own safety, but the mission was in jeopardy and he was determined not to fail. He would have to change the plan.

Towards evening they entered a village. So far, he had steered clear of any signs of habitation but they needed water and Lovell decided to take a chance. In the main square was an *abreuvoir* – a public cattle trough – and Lovell halted there to let horse and trooper drink their fill. He took a few gulps himself and washed his face. Then he unbuckled the saddlebags and hoisted them onto his shoulder. As an afterthought, he also untied his cape and draped it over the saddlebags.

A church spire was visible above the houses and he walked towards it. The village was very quiet. Like all French villages, it appeared deserted. A child peered at him from a doorway and a dog barked behind a gate. As he reached the church, the door opened and an elderly priest emerged.

'*Bonjour, mon père,*' Lovell said solemnly. '*Je suis un soldat anglais.*'

The old man examined the stranger closely. *Yes, a soldier,* he thought. *A strong man, but polite and humble.* He smiled sadly. '*Bonjour, monsieur.*'

'Father,' the Englishman continued in passable French, 'I need to pray.'

The priest nodded.

'Do you wish to confess, my son?'

Lovell shook his head.

'Thank you, father. I am not a Catholic. But may I enter your church?'

The old man made an expansive gesture. 'But of course. It is God's house.'

'*Merci bien, mon père.*'

'*Allez en paix, mon fils.*' The old man turned away and crossed the road to the *cure.*

Lovell entered the church and closed the door behind him. He stood for a moment, letting his eyes become accustomed to the dim light and making sure that he was alone. Then he strode quickly down the nave and found what he was looking for; to the left of the chancel were the steps and door to the crypt.

Ten minutes later, the priest watching from the window of the *cure* saw him emerge again from the church, his cape held loosely to his breast, his head bowed in contrition.

The old man nodded into his coffee bowl. Many strong men turned to God in times of war.

Lovell returned to the square where horse and trooper waited. The boy looked at him enquiringly but Lovell said nothing. He consulted his map briefly and put it away; he knew exactly where they were. They double-mounted and rode slowly down the main street; there was no urgency now.

As they passed the last of the buildings, the trooper turned and read the roadsign. It was the village of Flers.

PART 1

1

18 June 1916. Five thousand feet above Lens, the German air ace, Max Immelmann, glanced at the dashboard watch and pushed his Fokker monoplane into a dive. It was 8.59 p.m. Below him, in stepped-up 'V' formation, the seven mud-coloured biplanes flew steadily eastwards. They were British Type FEs: ungainly machines with a short, two-seater gondola backed by a skeleton fuselage and a rotary-driven pusher propeller. Their only defence was a single Lewis gun manned by the observer in the front cockpit. Immelmann had already destroyed an FE earlier in the day – his sixteenth victory – but half an hour ago, his celebratory dinner was interrupted by a report that even more of the enemy had crossed the front. Immelmann smiled grimly. The Englishmen would pay dearly for the interruption. He was invisible in the evening sun and thought he had a very good chance of getting one – possibly two – before they saw him.

His speed quickly brought him into position behind the two aircraft at the rear of the 'V'. He selected the one on the left and pulled back the cocking handles of his twin, forward-firing machine-guns. *Steady*, he said to himself. *Steady. Fire!* The Fokker shuddered and slowed from the recoil as the deadly Spandaus poured a hail of lead into the enemy machine. The FE staggered. Its propeller exploded in fragments and it dived earthwards.

'Seventeen!' Immelmann said aloud.

He kicked the rudder-bar and began to close on the right-hand machine. *Steady. Steady. Too late!* He'd been spotted. The Englishman flipped deftly onto his back and dived. *After him!* As his machine rolled gracefully after the fleeing aircraft, Immelmann saw the formation start to scatter.

The sleek Fokker caught the cumbersome FE easily. Immelmann closed to 50 metres. He'd always taken pride in getting close and using as little ammunition as possible. The FE filled his ring-sight. *Steady. Steady. Damn!* The Englishman had zoomed and started to climb. *Stay with him!* The biplane's greater wing-area took it up like a lift. Immelmann threw all his weight back on the stick and felt the force of the climb driving his blood into his boots. The two aircraft climbed steeper. Steeper. *Too steep!* The Fokker shuddered, stalled and fell away. *Damn!* Immelmann was livid. *Still seventeen! Never mind. Get home. Finish dinner. Seventeen today. Eighteen – perhaps nineteen – tomorrow.* Shudder. *What was that?* Something caught the corner of his eye and, turning his head, he watched incredulously as bullet holes began to appear in his port wing. Somehow the Englishman had got behind him and was attacking. *Dive! Use your speed!* Crash! Shudder. No feel in the stick. *Throttle Back! Can't. No control!* Power dive. Crash! as the tail breaks off. Crash! as the wings go. *Seventeen. Only seventeen.* The Fokker went into the ground at 200 m.p.h. At the last moment, Immelmann ducked his head instinctively. The dashboard watch, as it entered his skull, said 9 o'clock.

'How about that then, Charlie? I've got a Hun, and it's official.'

Corporal Waller grinned triumphantly up into the face of Sergeant Wren.

'Official Bollocks!' Wren sneered. 'You couldn't hit a barn door if you were standing on the step! Hawker got him with our fixed gun. When he went past you he was already going down. And if we weren't there he'd have had you for supper!'

'Oh piss off Charlie!' Waller retorted. 'You and Hawker aren't the only people who can get Huns. You should have the decency to admit that, this time, me and McCubbin beat you to it.'

The remaining six FE2s had returned to Allied lines and landed safely. The destruction of a Fokker fighter had cheered the men and the flight-debriefing had been a rowdy affair. Now the pilots had dispersed to their quarters and the observers trooped along to the armoury with their weapons and ammunition. They walked clumsily in leather coats and great sheepskin thigh-boots and carried the heavy Lewis guns on their shoulders, holding them by the barrel the way a navvy slings his hammer.

Wren stopped in his tracks and turned to face them.

'Wally,' he said with exaggerated patience, 'until you and all these other poor deluded bastards realise that you'll never hit anything with a flexible Lewis; until you give your pilot a fixed, forward-firing gun, we'll never be able to meet the Huns on equal terms. Look at that bloody fiasco at debriefing. One Hun takes on seven of us and knocks off Savage and Robinson before we even see him. Then Hawker gets him and it's: "Hooray! Jolly good show, chaps!" We've lost two men to their one and you'd think we'd won the war. It makes me bloody sick. I've a good mind to transfer back to the infantry. At least there you get credit where it's due.'

He turned again and continued to trudge disconsolately along the cinder path.

'Like hell you do!' Waller replied, hurrying to keep up.

'I've had that, too. And *I* got the Hun, Charlie, not *you*. If Hawker thought he'd got him, why didn't he say something when McCubbin claimed it?'

'Because he's too damned modest for his own good, that's why,' Wren replied over his shoulder. 'Hawker knows he's the best and he couldn't care less about keeping score. What he's interested in is improving standards in the squadron so that you lot can get Huns as well as us.'

This provoked a great roar of outrage from the following airmen and Wren ducked thankfully through the armoury doorway. He placed his Lewis gun and drums carefully on the counter in front of the armoury sergeant.

'Don't touch this one, Jonesy. I'll be down to see to it later.'

The armoury sergeant smiled. Wren's obsession with servicing his own gun was well known.

'Okay, Charlie, but you'd better get over to the CO's office. Lieutenant Hawker sent word for you to meet him there.'

'His master's voice,' Waller sneered.

Wren ignored the remark.

'Thanks, Jonesy,' he said cheerfully. 'I expect the medal's arrived at last. I wondered what was holding it up.'

He left the hut hurriedly, banging the door on the following hoots of derision. Secretly he was thinking: *What the hell do they want now?*

Second-Lieutenant Philip Hawker hurried along the path from the officers' quarters towards the squadron office. Two private soldiers coming towards him stepped off the path and saluted. Hawker, deep in thought, absently returned the salute and the men stepped back on the path. One said something to the other and they continued on their way, sniggering quietly.

It was a sad fact that Hawker's appearance amused people. He made an unlikely officer being short – five feet four – and skinny, and his face, dominated by big – usually grinning – buck-teeth was amazingly youthful. He had been in the Royal Flying Corps almost a year and should, officially, be about 19. Yet he looked much younger, and when he threw back his head and laughed loudly at one of his own jokes, he looked no more than 14 or 15.

Hawker's dress was typical of any young pilot. He wore the distinctive RFC 'maternity' tunic and Sam Browne belt and his Bedford cord breeches were tucked into golf stockings above a sturdy pair of brown brogues. He seldom worried about his appearance but this evening he had made a special effort. Smudges of cordite still showed like shadows beneath his ears and chin, but the front of his face was spotlessly clean. His shock of unruly fair hair had been subdued with a plastering of brilliantine and was crowned by an RFC forage cap.

The sound of a single aero engine rose and fell on the evening air and Hawker looked regretfully towards the great canvas Bessonneau hangars, where the riggers and engine fitters were preparing the aircraft for another day's work. He had been less than satisfied with the performance of his engine after the scrap with the Hun and he had particularly wanted to be there when the fitters took it down. Hawker had every confidence in the men, but engines thrilled and fascinated him and he always liked to see things for himself. Instead, he had been summoned to Major Shaw's office to meet an important visitor and, as he walked along, he wondered who it could be.

Hawker's frown of concern gave way to a smile of recognition as he spotted Charlie Wren hurrying along from the Sergeants' quarters looking equally discomforted. Their paths converged as they approached the offices and Hawker grinned mischievously.

19

'Best bib and tucker, Charlie?' he said.

Wren was a famous grouser.

Wren refused to smile. He had been partnering Hawker for six months now and, though he had a high regard for Hawker's abilities as a fighting pilot, the constant exuberance and schoolboy humour sometimes wore a bit thin.

Hawker shook his head in exasperation.

'Charlie, you're not still sulking over my letting old McCubbin claim that Hun, are you?'

'No, sir.'

'Good,' Hawker said.

'But I still don't understand why you did it,' Wren persisted. 'You know perfectly well that you were the one who got him. When we were scrapping, the rest of the flight were scattering like a bunch of old women. The Hun just happened to fall past Mr McCubbin when he was going down.'

'Apparently McCubbin's man got a good shot at him,' Hawker said.

'Was that before or after the wings fell off?' Wren replied sarcastically.

Hawker laughed delightedly.

'We've had all this out before, Charlie. It doesn't really matter who got the Hun. The main thing is that the squadron will get the credit for it and all the chaps will be encouraged. The adjutant said the Old Man was very pleased. He said: "This proves that the FE is a match for any damned Hun. Now our chaps can really teach those Fokkers a lesson!"' Hawker grinned shyly. 'At least, I *think* that's what he said.'

Wren smiled grudgingly. The Old Man's penchant for strong language was known to officers and men alike.

'And that's the point, Charlie,' Hawker continued. 'The Fokker's reputation has been completely overblown. It's fast in a dive but in manoeuvre it has all the qualities of a house brick. You and I know that, so we know how to deal with it. Now we've started shooting them down, the message will get through to the other chaps.'

'But they won't achieve anything with a flexible gun, sir,' Wren pointed out.

Hawker smiled.

'No, they won't. But gradually they'll begin to see. Once they have the confidence to scrap with the Huns, the pilots will soon catch on that they could achieve a lot more with a fixed, forward-firing gun. *Then*, and this is the main point,' Hawker stressed, '*then* they'll adopt the idea with enthusiasm because they'll have thought of it themselves.' Hawker grinned and tapped his head with a forefinger. 'Psychology, Charlie. That's the way to do it. Trust me. In a few weeks the entire squadron will be using fixed guns.'

If there's any squadron left by then, Wren thought. But he gave it up. You couldn't out-talk Hawker. And besides, they had reached the two adjoining wooden huts that served as the squadron offices.

Hawker knocked and they entered. In the outer office, Captain Wilson, the adjutant and recording officer, sat at a desk covered in papers. The room was full of tobacco smoke and Hawker who was a non-smoker, coughed involuntarily.

'Gad, Jock, when was this den last raided?' he protested.

Wilson grinned, removed the pipe from his face and waved it at some tired cane chairs standing against the wall.

'Take a pew, chaps, the Old Man's busy at present. Look at this lot,' he added, indicating the mass of papers. 'This is the paperwork on Savage and Robinson. If you chaps realised the extra work it causes me, you'd be a bit more careful about getting yourselves shot down.'

'It sounds as if they might have got away with it though,' Hawker said earnestly. 'They were both conscious when they were going down.'

'Let's hope so,' Wilson replied. 'Even so, they're into the bag for the duration. Something not to be relished. I knew a chap once . . .' He broke off as the door of the inner office opened and Major Shaw stuck his head out. 'There you are, chaps. You can come in now. And bring the chairs, would you.'

He held the door as they filed through carrying their chairs.

A man in colonel's uniform sat with his back to them, facing the CO's desk. As they entered, he rose and moved his own chair so that he sat at the far end of the desk.

As he did so, Hawker exclaimed in recognition, 'Hello, sir! What brings you to the squadron again?'

Colonel Sir John Trent held out his hand.

'Good to see you again, Hawker,' he said gruffly.

Wren was a little slow on the uptake but when he saw who it was, his hopes of leave or even of a reasonably quiet life went straight out the window.

'Sergeant.'

Sir John generously extended his hand to Wren in turn. The hand was soft and warm.

'Good evening, sir, 'Wren said guardedly.

It was the uniform that had thrown Wren. The last time they had met, Sir John had been in civilian clothes. However, nowadays it was probably considered impolitic for civil servants to wander around northern France in mufti, so Sir John had availed himself of uniform and rank. *Just like that*, thought Wren who, despite his worldly cynicism, took a certain pride in his rank and uniform. His resentment sought an outlet in words.

'Congratulations, sir. It's a grand life!' he said cheerfully.

Sir John frowned.

'The uniform, sir,' Wren prompted. 'You've joined up since we last met.'

No one was taken in. Hawker suppressed a smile. Sir

John continued to frown and Major Shaw looked at Wren sternly. 'That'll do, Sergeant,' he snapped.

Wren grinned. 'May we smoke, sir?'

The major deferred to Sir John, who assented.

'Of course. Feel free.'

Wren didn't move and the Major glared and pushed a packet of Goldflake across the desk towards him. Wren selected one of the fat white tubes, struck a match and inhaled luxuriously.

'Thank you very much, sir.'

He squinted through the smoke at Sir John and remembered the last time they had met.

It had been five months ago at the end of January when Sir John Trent's outfit, an obscure department of the British Secret Service, had been convinced that the Germans were planning an attack on the French fortress town of Verdun. The French high command would have none of it, believing that the enemy's offensive would occur on the Champagne front. Sir John had therefore hatched a plan to send two British airmen behind German lines to gain proof of the coming attack. Hawker and Wren had done the job but it was a crazy plan and they had barely escaped with their lives.* In short, the presence of Sir John Trent, in or out of uniform, spelt trouble.

'Right then.' Major Shaw called an impatient end to the preliminaries. 'Let's get on. Sir John, would you like to put them in the picture?'

'Certainly.' Sir John settled himself in his chair, smiled grimly at each of his listeners in turn, and began to speak. 'I'll start at the beginning. As you all know, the first thing a nation must do in times of national danger is secure its wealth, especially gold bullion reserves, art treasures and crown jewels. In the case of threatened invasion, treasures

* See *Hawker's War*

23

are often moved out of the country – to safe colonies, friendly countries – that sort of thing.

'This safeguarding of the nation's wealth will even take precedence over the safety of citizens, rather in the manner of a wealthy householder who, perceiving his house is on fire, will first save his valuables in the belief that it would be preferable for he and his family to perish in the flames rather than be condemned to a life of penury. And so it was that when Germany announced its intention to invade Belgium, King Albert immediately ordered all national treasures to be moved away – to neutral Holland, to Paris and, via the various channel ports, to London. This was accomplished swiftly and effectively.' Sir John nodded. 'It was a prudent move. Now their Belgian majesties, living in a fishing village in the last free corner of their beloved country, at least know they have the means to rebuild when the Germans are finally driven out.

'But, of course, in such cases of swift action, small but significant things are sometimes forgotten. Our wealthy gentleman, as he watches his house collapse in flames suddenly remembers his grandfather's watch – a family heirloom – is still in the bedside cabinet. Or the lady of the house wistfully realises the packet of love letters that have lain for years in the back of her linen drawer have gone forever. And so it was with Belgium. In Brussels a prominent jeweller, frantically re-checking his lists, realised with despair that pieces of jewellery sent for specialist cleaning and repair had not been returned by the technician in Mons. Several of the items belonged to the Royal Family and there was a necklace particularly beloved by Queen Elisabeth.

'The jeweller was frantic. He had several times personally waited on their majesties himself; with the jewels missing, how could he ever face them again? And most of his high-class clientele came to him solely because it was known that

24

he had royal patronage. He immediately telephoned the workshop of the technician – no reply. He tried the technician's home number – and was in luck. The technician sought to reassure his client. Yes, Mons was being evacuated. Refugees were streaming south. Even the British soldiers sent to defend the town were pulling out. The technician's family had already left to stay with relatives in France. But *Monsieur* had no need to worry. The jewels were quite safe in a hidden vault below the basement of the house. The vault was fireproof and its entrance was invisible from the cellar. Even if the house was occupied by Germans or razed to the ground, the jewels would still be safe. Furthermore the existence of the vault was known only to the technician, his wife and his eldest son.

'The jeweller couldn't believe his ears. "Idiot," he raged. "Dolt! You have just told *me* of the vault's existence! How many more clients have you told to reassure them?" "Believe me, sir," the technician whined, "the jewels are safe." "No!" said the jeweller. "You will wait there. I will send someone to collect the jewels." "But, sir," the technician pleaded, "my lists are with my wife who has already left for France. Without my lists, I can't be sure of identifying all the royal pieces. All the jewels are together in the same safe." "Then," said the jeweller, "you will hand all the gems over to the people I send. Those jewels which are not royal will be returned to you in due course. If you do not do this, you will answer to the King himself. Furthermore, I will see to it that you will never work in the trade again." '

Sir John snorted ironically and grinned at his listeners.

'It may well be that the jeweller will come to wish he had left the treasure where it was.' Sir John had finished his cigarette. He removed the stub from the end of his holder, replaced it from a gold case and offered the case to the Major and Wren. They all lit up and Sir John continued.

'The jeweller was a prominent, international businessman

and had many high ranking contacts all over Europe. Within half an hour he was in telephone contact with Sir John French, whose British Expeditionary Force was in process of vacating Mons. Within the hour, a captain and a small detachment of the Royal Scots Greys was on the technician's doorstep with written orders to collect the "merchandise". Their secret mission was to carry the jewels to the Channel and hand them over to the Captain of a Royal Navy destroyer, who would then deliver them to England.'

'I say, sir!' Hawker exclaimed. 'This is like something out of the *Boy's Own Paper*!'

Sir John nodded.

'It is indeed. And I'm afraid there's more to come. At this point, it might be appropriate to reveal to you the identity of the Scots Greys' captain. It was Captain Lord Rupert Lovell. You may have heard of him. He . . .'

Sir John broke off at an audible gasp from Hawker who appeared to be having some kind of fit. He sat bolt upright in his chair, grasping the arms so that his knuckles showed white; while his eyes, riveted on Sir John, stood out like organ stops. 'Did you say Rupert Lovell, sir?' Hawker finally yelped in disbelief.

'That's what I said,' Sir John replied airily.

'*The* Rupert Lovell,' Hawker persisted. 'Lovell the jockey, Lovell the racing driver, Lovell of the North-West Frontier?'

'I take it you've heard of him.'

Sir John smiled dryly.

'Heard of him, sir! He's been my absolute hero since I saw him driving the Napier Six at Brooklands in 1910. I actually met him once in the car park at Aintree. He was driving the Delage Ten that he raced in the 1912 *Coupe de l'Auto* at Boulogne. I went up to him and shook his hand. Of course, I was very young then,' Hawker said sheepishly. 'My father was livid but old Lovell was as nice as nine-pence.

Showed me over the car and everything. Then he went out and rode the winner of the Grand Military Chase. I had five bob on it myself; a whole month's pocket money. It was the most exciting day of my life!'

Sir John smiled indulgently.

'Well, Hawker, I think you've just about summed up Lord Lovell. But for the benefit of those without your detailed knowledge of the sporting scene, perhaps you'd allow me to continue.'

'Captain Lord Rupert Lovell,' Sir John began, 'is the only child – and the heir of course – of Lord Peter, the 6th Earl of Blaney. He was born at the family seat, Blaney Hall, in Blaney, a small mining and mill town in Yorkshire. He was educated at Wellington and Sandhurst. While at Sandhurst, he was a notable sportsman: rowing, shooting, point-to-point, motor-car racing – a hell of a competitor! On passing out of Sandhurst, he was commissioned into the Indian Army and joined the family regiment, the Rajputana Rifles. However, always in search of action, he soon transferred to the Frontier Force Regiment and spent two years dashing around the North-West Frontier, bashing Baluchis and punishing Pathans . . .'

Sir John broke off as Hawker laughed delightedly. Sir John nodded and smiled ruefully.

'Well, you know the kind of thing. Apparently, while on the Frontier he dropped out of sight for a while. But he eventually reappeared and there were strong rumours that he'd been a politico in Afghanistan, living with the nomadic tribesmen and keeping an eye on the Russians.' Sir John chuckled. 'He also acquired the tribesman's penchant for cold steel. It seems he's an absolute devil with a Khyber Knife; still carries one here in France. Of course, being such a colourful character, he's acquired several nicknames. At Sandhurst he was known as Lovell the Dog, partly because Lovell greyhounds dominated the Waterloo Cup around

27

the turn of the century, and partly after the old Tudor propaganda rhyme.'

Here Hawker interrupted, reciting in a mock-Shakespearean falsetto: '*The cat, the rat and Lov-ell the dog, ruled all England under the hog.*'

'That's the one,' Sir John said patiently. 'In India, his fellow officers called him "Mad" Lovell, because he was prone to acts of derring-do and after *Mad Carew* in the *Little Yellow God* poem.

'*He returned before the dawn, With his shirt and tunic torn, And a gash across his temples dripping red!*' Hawker cried dramatically.

'That's the one,' Sir John sighed.

'Hawker, shut up and pay attention!' Major Shaw roared, his eyes blazing

'Sorry, sir.' Hawker hung his head.

Sir John continued.

'My reason for giving you this fairly detailed history of Captain Lovell is to demonstrate that if Sir John French had had his pick of all the officers in the British Army, he could hardly have come up with a more gallant, reliable and trustworthy gentleman than the one who happened to be on hand at the time. However, on this vital occasion Captain Lovell's luck failed to hold out. He was intent on avoiding trouble but you must remember that northern France at that time was a very chaotic place. No one quite knew the exact positions of allies and enemies and Lovell's little group had to cross many miles of potentially hostile territory. After a brush with the enemy which lost one of their number, they were shelled by artillery, unidentified but probably French batteries at Peronne, that mistook them for marauding Uhlans.'

'I say, bad show!' Hawker exclaimed.

Sir John nodded sadly.

'Precisely. It was a very bad show indeed. Three more

men killed. Horses killed and scattered. Only Captain Lovell and a single wounded trooper remained to escape on one horse. The jewels also had to be carried by the same tired animal. Captain Lovell was concerned that in their weakened state and on a single horse they were in grave danger of being overtaken by the Germans. He had no knowledge of how far westwards von Kluck's army had advanced. Perhaps there were already scouting columns between himself and the Channel. He therefore decided to play safe and hide the treasure to stop it falling into German hands. He reasoned that, whatever happened, as long as he survived the jewels could be recovered.'

Sir John smiled broadly.

'Happily both men *did* survive. Captain Lovell would have received the Victoria Cross for getting the wounded trooper back, but he flatly refused it. You see, he concluded that he had failed in his mission and betrayed the King of Belgium's trust. He therefore took an oath to refuse all honours or promotion until the treasure had been recovered. Now it looks as if conditions are at last right for this to be accomplished. And you chaps are to have the privilege of helping Captain Lovell fulfil his solemn oath.'

'I say!' Hawker gasped excitedly.

Oh balls, Wren thought despairingly. *Here we go again.*

2

Sir John Trent hesitated. He picked up his gold cigarette case and stared into its dull lustre as if seeking inspiration. At last he laid it aside and looked keenly at his audience.

'I have already explained how Captain Lovell was forced to hide the jewels he was taking to the coast. Only he and I know their exact location, but we believe there will shortly be a genuine chance to recover the treasure.'

Sir John took a deep breath.

'Gentlemen, it is time for plain speaking. As you all know, the British Army on the Somme is about to attack. The "Big Push" is about to begin!'

The listening group were astonished at the colonel's frank statement but he looked them in the face and shrugged helplessly.

'The roads are full of transport columns; fifteen hundred guns are in place; two million shells have been stockpiled. Fourth Army has sixteen fighting divisions – half-a-million men. Water pipes are being laid; telephone lines buried; assault trenches dug. The Royal Flying Corps is doing its best to knock down Hun balloons and observation aircraft, but the secret can no longer be hidden. We know it; the men know it; the Germans know it. Yesterday, the Huns in Beaumont Hamel put up a notice board. It said: "Good luck in your coming attack."

'The only thing none of us knows is the exact date. But it

will be very soon. We're ready! And although the Germans know the attack is coming, they can't do anything about it. As soon as the weather improves and the gunners can see what they're hitting, a massive bombardment will fall on the German front line. This will continue for five days. On the morning of the sixth day, the attack will begin. By that time, most of the defending Germans will be dead or buried alive in their dugouts. After five days of continuous bombardment, the few that are left will be in no fit state to resist. Our troops will go over with full packs and plenty of ammunition and equipment to withstand counter-attacks. The artillery will then shift its attention to the German rear areas. Our supporting troops will pass through the captured first line and attack the second and third lines. When these are breached, the cavalry will go through and there will be a general advance towards Cambrai.'

Sir John smiled.

'These are the conditions that will enable Captain Lovell to recover the jewels. He needs to get to the village of Flers (he pronounced it 'Flairs'), which of course is behind German lines and has been for two years. In the coming attack, our second objective after occupying the German front line, is to seize the high ground between Bapaume and Ginchy. We should overrun Flers in about three days, but Captain Lovell wants to reach the village before our advance brings it into the front line – that is before it is reduced to rubble by our artillery. Therefore, just before the main attack begins, he intends to lead a small party *behind* the German lines, reach Flers, recover the jewels and go to ground until the village is occupied by our troops.'

The colonel paused and chuckled at the expressions on their faces. Even Major Shaw's registered astonishment and doubt, with a hint of relief that he himself would take no part in the proceedings.

'Normally, of course,' Sir John continued, 'a special

31

operation like this would not be permitted in the middle of a major attack, when all efforts should be subservient to the main objective. However, my minister has talked to the C.-in-C. and Sir Douglas has reluctantly allowed the operation to go ahead in the interests of Anglo-Belgian relations. But there is a price! The operation must also make a direct contribution to the "Big Push". Captain Lovell will explain this to you later. By happy coincidence, one of units in the front line is the 1st Battalion of the Blaney Pals. This battalion will attack on the left of the line towards one of the German strong points, the fortified village of Serre. As I've explained, Captain Lovell has strong family connections with Blaney and the Pals have agreed to help his party pass through the German line. They already have a plan for this worked out.'

Sir John grinned and spread his hands in a gesture of finality.

'Well, gentlemen, that's it! You now know as much as I. Major Shaw has kindly agreed to release you from your squadron duties for as long as this job takes and Captain Lovell will send for you shortly. I suggest you lay off flying for a few days, get plenty of exercise and prepare yourselves for life with the infantry. Any questions?'

Charlie Wren sat in dumbfounded silence. The question screaming in his brain was: *Why me?* Then he smiled in surprise as Hawker spoke.

'Why us, sir?' Hawker asked innocently.

The colonel frowned.

'How do you mean, Lieutenant?'

Hawker blushed with embarrassment.

'I mean, this is a wizard scheme, sir, and Sergeant Wren and I are honoured to be asked, but . . .'

He broke off at Wren's snort of amusement. It was obvious that they weren't being *asked.*

Wren resumed a straight face as Major Shaw looked at him sharply.

'What I mean, sir,' Hawker went on, 'is while we'll be happy and honoured to accompany Captain Lovell on his mission, how did he happen to choose us? I mean, Captain Lovell is a national hero; he doesn't know we exist.'

Sir John smiled patiently.

'Lieutenant, this business of the jewels is a very sensitive issue and potentially one of great embarrassment to us in our relations with our Belgian allies. My department has been engaged since the jewels first failed to arrive in London. When Captain Lovell outlined his plan to recover them I realised we would have to pick the team very carefully. We need men who are completely trustworthy, with initiative and a proven ability to operate behind enemy lines. I immediately thought of you and the sergeant here. I told Captain Lovell that you had twice done valuable work for my department and that you were ideal men for the job. He agreed to your going along on the condition that he could also take one of his own men; his batman, would you believe? I saw no real objection to that, and concurred.'

Hawker beamed with pleasure.

'Thank you very much, sir. We'll do our best not to let you down.'

Sir John smiled and nodded.

'I know you will, Lieutenant. Now you'd better get along.'

Hawker and Wren rose, picked up their chairs and filed out of the office.

'Goodbye, sir,' Hawker said as he closed the door behind him.

'Goodbye, ' the colonel replied. 'And good luck to you both.'

Sir John grinned at the closed door and glanced shrewdly at Major Shaw.

'I hope I've done right in sending that sergeant along on a mission like this,' he said. 'Those jewels are worth a fortune.'

He had noted that, from the time he had started to explain the mission, Wren hadn't uttered a word.

'Sergeant Wren is very capable, sir,' Major Shaw replied earnestly.

Sir John chuckled.

'That's what worries me. I should think he's capable of anything! Still,' he added more soberly, 'they've got a hell of a task ahead of them and I can't think of any two men more likely to succeed. They did a damn fine job for me at Verdun!'

The colonel stood up and made to leave, but Major Shaw remained seated and appeared deep in thought. When Sir John paused and looked at him, the major stirred himself and turned up a worried face.

'Sir John,' the major blurted out at last, 'what's going to happen? Will the "Big Push" succeed; will we in fact break through?'

Sir John shrugged impatiently.

'I don't know. No one knows. It may succeed completely and end the war. With all the hard work and planning, it certainly deserves to succeed.'

'But off the record,' Major Shaw persisted. 'In your own personal opinion, Sir John. Is that likely to happen?'

There was a compelling intensity in the major's voice and Sir John sat back in his chair again, took out his case and lit another cigarette. He inhaled hugely and expelled the smoke in a great sigh. He looked at the major levelly.

'The attack can succeed, and it may succeed in its entirety.'

'But . . .,' the major prompted.

Sir John shrugged

'But the Germans are very strong. They're not fools and

34

they've had almost two years to prepare their defences. Three lines of defences. We may break through all along the front, but more probably we'll break through in places. The *Boche* will counter-attack and pinch off some of the advances. In others we'll repel them and make some gains. In any case it doesn't really matter. This offensive is not about beating the Germans outright; it's about saving the French. We have to convince them that we are prepared to pay the same price on the Somme as they are paying at Verdun. We must stop them losing heart and preserve the Alliance.

'To divert German troops away from the Meuse, the French have demanded a joint attack astride the River Somme and we have had to comply. We can't fight this war on our own; we have to keep the French on side. There is now only one sure key to victory – attrition. All the nations involved have huge citizen armies. They have millions of men and are prepared to sacrifice them. If one nation were to say: "Enough! We are civilised people. We will no longer send our young men to certain death in their thousands," then that nation will lose the war. If ourselves or the French were to say that and seek peace on German terms, a large part of France would remain in German hands and Belgium would cease to exist. Those lost territories would become part of a greater Germany. Russia, on her own, would be powerless and the new German empire would stretch from the English Channel to the Ukraine.

'Can you imagine that, Major? A German empire ruled by the Kaiser, flush with victory and madder than ever!' Sir John shook his head emphatically. 'No. It's a nightmare and it can't be allowed to happen. No matter what it costs, Britain will pay the required price on the Somme. And it won't stop there. It will go on and on.'

Sir John removed the remains of his cigarette from its holder and stubbed it out in the ashtray.

As he listened to the colonel's prognosis, Major Hart's face had registered first unease and then a growing horror.

At last, he could contain himself no longer and burst out in protest, 'But that's terrible!'

Sir John looked up in surprise

The major recovered himself and tried to speak more reasonably.

'I beg your pardon, Sir John, but what you are suggesting is appalling. Hundreds of thousands of our people marching to their deaths. Can the nation sustain it? What will happen in the end?'

'Germany will break,' the colonel replied mildly. 'If Britain, France and Russia hold firm and continue to pay the price, the Huns can't win. In the numbers game we have the advantage. It's as simple as that. And as long as we remember that, all will be well.'

'Well!' Major Shaw echoed in exasperation. You call it "well". I find it a dreadful prospect!'

Sir John chuckled at the other's discomfort.

'Oh come now, Major, it's not as bad as all that. Don't forget the Huns know all this too. It's been gnawing at their clever, Teutonic brains since the beginning, when they hacked through Belgium in a desperate bid for a quick victory – and failed. Because what the Germans fear above all is a war on two fronts. They know that if they can't break the Allied nerve, the numbers are against them and they're bound to lose.'

Sir John glanced at his wristwatch and stood up. He shrugged into his greatcoat and picked up his briefcase and cap. Finally, the major too rose from the table and accompanied his guest to the door. He still appeared preoccupied and moved slowly as if weighed down by some burden. At the door, Sir John turned and looked at the other keenly.

'Major, you must believe me when I tell you that, whatever happens, the "Big Push" on the Somme will change the course of the war. It will be very gratifying if the German line is broken, if the cavalry goes through and there is a general advance to Cambrai. But whether the attack succeeds in all its ambition is really immaterial. The true objective of this attack, and of all others, is to kill as many Germans as possible.'

3

Lord Kitchener was dead, drowned when the cruiser taking him on a secret mission to Russia struck a mine in the North Sea and sank within 15 minutes. Kitchener was gone but he had left a legacy: a new volunteer army of two million men.

This citizen army encountered no culture shock on arriving in France. Royal Navy transports delivered them to the ports of Calais, Le Havre and Boulogne which, with their forests of cranes and tide-ravaged beaches, were no different from any port in the world. The soldiers detrained at railheads christened Lime Street and Kings Cross, and slogged up to the lines along trenches sign posted Sauchiehall Street, Bramall Lane and Piccadilly. Even the unpronounceable French towns in which they were billeted were easily adapted: Mailly Maillet became 'Milly Mallet', Auchonvillers 'Ocean Villas' and Sailly-au-Bois simply 'Sally'. In the front line the men looked out on 'Flatiron Copse', 'Bailiff Wood' and 'Sausage Valley'.

The British found Picardy to be much like Wiltshire or Kent. It was downy, chalk country. Thrushes sang in the hedgerows and poppies and cornflowers grew on the banks of sunken lanes. In June the fields were green with beet and potatoes and high, ripening corn.

Soldiers of the new army were, for the most part, happy with their lot. They relished the exercise and sunshine and the three meals a day fed them by a doting nation. The majority were Kitchener volunteers, proud and thankful that they had got into the army in time for the 'Big Push' that would teach the Hun a lesson and kick his backside out of France and Belgium.

'Old army' men, few now since Wipers, Loos and Neuve Chapelle, tended to keep their heads down. They were uneasy before all this enthusiasm and confidence. They had seen what machine-gun fire had done to their mates and what high explosive could do to the best of soldiers. Those that hadn't managed to work their tickets back to 'home establishment' crossed their fingers, knocked on wood and waited in trepidation for the next 'show'. They knew their best chance was for a 'Blighty touch'; not a big wound but one serious enough to get them out of the front line for good. Lost fingers or a mild 'gassing' were small prices to pay for a long life and an end to squalor. But old soldiers acquire a knack of living from day to day. They are, by nature, optimists. They survived before and may do so again. And anyway – it might never happen!

In such frame of mind, one old soldier drove confidently into the main square of the town of Albert. Charlie Wren had decided that if he was to take part in another hare-brained Secret Service scheme, he would make sure he had the right tackle for the job. He had therefore come to collect a special purchase from an old Army Service Corps contact.

He had his directions from an ASC driver: *Go to the church in the main square. From the hanging virgin, walk towards the railway station. It's the last street on the left – Roo Emily Zola.*

Wren parked the Crossley tender and looked up at the shell-damaged spire of the big church. From the very top of the spire, the golden statue of the Virgin and Child still hung precariously over the street. Before she was toppled, the Virgin had held the child high above her head to show

39

the world the new Saviour. Now, as she hung above the square at an angle of 30 degrees, it appeared that the precious child had fallen and the Virgin had dived head first to save him. The damage to the spire had been caused in the first months of the war and a legend had spread through the army that when Virgin and Child finally fell, the war would end.

As Wren walked briskly towards the railway station he was alert to any sound of incoming shells. The station, he knew, no longer received trains. Rail traffic from the coast and Amiens terminated down the line at Buire-sur-l'Ancre, but the town still suffered sporadic attention from German long-range guns and the buildings around him had been badly damaged. Rue Émile Zola duly appeared on the left and Wren soon found the robust cellar that served as Sergeant Webb's underground 'store'.

Quarter-Master Sergeant 'Spider' Webb had already made a small fortune out of the war and was industriously building a bigger one. He boasted that, given time, he could supply anything to anyone. ASC lorry drivers delivered Webb's goods throughout Northern France. He had contacts in every area of commerce and enjoyed the backing of several London banks. He had accounts with Harrods and Fortnum & Mason; with Ladbrokes; and with the all the leading tailors and shirt makers. With Spider you could order a hamper, place a bet, book a box at Ascot or buy an outfit for any occasion. He had no regard for rank or position. He would deal with companies, regiments and brigades; or individuals: commissioned, non-commissioned and private. He demanded only one courtesy – cash on delivery.

Wren announced himself to one of the clerks and Spider eventually emerged from the inner office looking weary but philosophical beneath his immense burden of trade. When he saw Wren, he put on his professional smile – an brief

40

upturn of his thin mouth – before the solemn duty of bargaining and business. He regarded Wren warily having dealt with him before; Wren assumed his usual air of studied cynicism.

Spider fetched a slim, heavy-looking object from the back room.

It was wrapped in a soft cloth and tied with string. 'I've got just the article you ordered, Charlie. You're going to like this.'

He untied the string and carefully unwrapped the package. Inside was an ugly, single-barrelled shotgun.

Wren picked it up disconsolately.

'This is no good,' he said. 'I asked for a double. A single's no good at all.'

'This is better than a double, Charlie,' Webb said eagerly. He took the weapon from Wren and brought it to his shoulder. The gun had a looped lever behind the trigger guard and Spider expertly worked the action. 'It's a repeater. Winchester Model 87, designed for railway guards in the States. Look here.'

He pointed to an engraving on the gun's receiver. It said: 'AM EX CO'.

'See that? American Express Company. This is just what you want, Charlie.'

Wren took the shotgun back.

'I dunno,' he said doubtfully. 'With a sawn-off double everyone knows what you've got. You fire one and the second one's a threat.'

'I know what you *mean*, Charlie,' Spider said with a salesman's patience. 'A sawn-off packs a punch, you can swing it in a small space and you can hide it under your coat. But it's a make-shift. It's a cut-down sporting piece. This here is tailor-made for the job. With this you can clear a trench or dugout single handed. Look at this.' He held up one of the Winchester's cartridges. 'These aren't bird or

41

buckshot. This is Double-O: nine pellets to a shell. Close up they blow a hole in a man as big as your fist. Six shots – five in the magazine and one up the pipe. This is the business, Charlie. I'd take it if I were you.'

'How much?' Wren asked.

'To you, twenty quid.'

'I don't want to *buy*,' Wren said casually, anticipating the reaction. 'How much to hire – for a week?'

'Hire?' Webb said indignantly. 'I don't hire. I sell stuff!'

'You're behind the times then,' Wren said seriously. 'Hire's the thing nowadays. All the top businessmen are into hire.'

'Why?' Spider asked dazedly.

'Because you make money and you've still got the merchandise.'

As Spider grappled with this profound thought, Wren pressed home his advantage.

'I'll pay you a fiver for a week's use. I'd take it if I were you.'

He put down a five pound note and gathered up the cloth and the box of cartridges.

Webb made a grab to retrieve his property.

'What if you don't come back?' he whined.

'If I don't come back, you can keep this,' Wren said. He unhooked the holstered Luger from his belt and handed it over. 'I'll leave you this as a deposit.'

Spider examined the pistol and licked his lips greedily.

'Five quid and this?' he said, unable to keep the satisfaction out of his voice.

Wren grinned.

'Five quid,' he said. 'I'll be back for the pistol.'

Wren stowed his purchase in his haversack and climbed the cellar steps back into daylight. He had heard that elements of the Blaney Pals were billeted in Albert and he thought that this was an ideal time to get acquainted with

42

his new commander. After several enquiries and false starts he finally located the cellar that was Captain Lovell's quarters. Wren knocked hard on the wood panelling of the stairway.

'Come in,' a voice called tetchily.

Wren descended and stepped off the stairs into a large, warm room. A variety of thick rugs covered the floor; there was a smell of paraffin and the room was lit by several oil lamps. Captain Lord Lovell did himself well. As his eyes grew accustomed to the light, Wren saw a small, bent figure polishing a pair of boots in a corner. It made no move to acknowledge him.

'Is Captain Lovell around?' Wren demanded at last.

The man stopped his polishing and looked ponderously about him.

'Can't see him?' he replied sarcastically. Then he rose suddenly and squinted in the poor light. 'Who's that? I know you, don't I?'

And as the lamplight fell on the man's face, Wren too stared in recognition.

'Good God! Jacko Bass!' He laughed aloud in surprise. 'So this is what you've come to, Jacko. War's a terrible thing!' he added, grinning.

'Hello, Charlie,' The man replied grumpily. 'What brings you here?'

Bass was a short, wiry man with an outsized head. His pinched, worried face was born of a lifelong struggle against fate and his own weakness. He was prematurely bald and had a large, hooked nose and big ears. His mouth was wide and thin. It was the unpainted face of a clown. Wren knew him from Civvy Street. Handicapped by his poor beginnings, he had served time for burglary and petty theft; but he had above-average intelligence and a rare gift with figures. He had found regular employment as a bookmaker's clerk. Wren always had a liking for the little man.

He was harmless and his mobile, expressive face made people laugh.

'I'm looking for Captain Lovell,' Wren said. 'What're you, his batman?'

'No, I'm Field-Marshall Haig dropped in for a chat,' Bass replied morosely. 'The Captain's gone to Amiens. He won't be back for hours.'

'That suits me,' Wren said. He threw his cap into a corner and slumped into a wooden, wheel-backed armchair. 'How about a drink, Jacko?'

'I don't know,' Bass replied resentfully, 'I'm not sure I fancy a drink with you.'

'You're joking!' Wren's said. 'Why wouldn't a nice bloke like you not want to drink with a nice bloke like me?'

'Because, Charlie,' Bass said evenly, 'the last time we met we weren't drinking. The last time we met you were punching my bloody lights out!'

'That wasn't my fault,' Wren said. 'That was business.'

'Some bloody business!' Bass replied hotly. 'You cracked three of my ribs!'

'You'd been a naughty boy,' Wren said mildly. 'My boss Solly Nyman lost a lot of money. Somebody had to pay. You just happened to be there at the time.'

'Somebody's got to get beaten up every time Solly takes a loss?' Jacko said indignantly.

'When it's crooked, yes.'

'What was crooked about it?' Bass said sullenly.

'Everything!' Wren replied with a laugh. 'Don't give me that bollocks, Jacko. You were in it up to your neck. Don't tell me you've forgotten the Peter Piper business, because I won't believe you.'

'I remember the bets,' Bass said stiffly. 'They were big.'

'They were,' Wren replied ironically. 'With good reason. Peter Piper ran at Newmarket in a Handicap Plate for 3-year-olds. He won by a street at 8–1. The trouble was, the horse that ran wasn't Peter Piper at all. He was switched for a ringer in a pull-in on the Cambridge Road. The horse that ran in his place was Voltigeur Shamrock, a 4-year-old trained in Ireland. Your boss, Morry Silver, knew all about the switch but instead of telling Solly about it, he laid off everything he had with him. You should know,' Wren added accusingly. 'You were the one who phoned it through.'

Bass nodded and grinned crookedly.

'I was', he admitted, 'but I was only doing what I was told. I'd laid off a monkey with Greek Tony and told him to pass it on. And Morry said: "Give a monkey to Solly Nyman, only don't tell him to get rid of it. Tell you what, make it a grand; I'll have a monkey on for myself; that makes it personal." Then he started laughing and coughing fit to bust. He hated Solly's guts for some reason.'

'The feeling was mutual,' Wren said grimly. 'When Solly heard what had happened, he went doolally. He called me in and said: "Charlie, get up to the Prince of Wales on Lea Bridge Road. Morry always calls in there on his way home. Get over there and teach that bloody toe-rag some business manners." But when we got there he'd gone and we had to make do with you. It was bad luck on you but somebody had to pay.'

'Even so,' Bass said resentfully, 'you needn't have been so keen about it. You cracked three of my ribs. I was in bloody agony for weeks.'

'You can't help ribs.' Wren said philosophically. 'They either break or they don't. And you're forgetting who was with me that night. Terry Violet. "*Clogger*" Violet. He wore steel-capped boots. I didn't want you to have a rough time, so I said: "This one's mine, Terry. You had the last one." And while he was trying to remember who the last one was, I started giving you the business. Then you started yelling and somebody threw a bottle and a whole rumpus started. I grabbed hold of Terry and we slipped out the back. All the

45

way home, Terry was moaning that he hadn't panned anybody. You got off light,' Wren said in conclusion, 'and I reckon you owe me a drink.'

'All right,' Bass assented. 'But it'll have to be beer. I can have as much beer as I like as long as I stay sober, but he won't let me touch the spirits.'

'Very wise,' Wren replied. 'Beer'll be fine.'

Bass sauntered over to a corner of the room where a variety of crates containing bottles of all descriptions were stacked. He selected a quart bottle of Pale Ale and took two glasses from a chest on the floor. He poured beer into each and sat down again, handing one of the glasses to Wren. He opened a new packet of Players, threw one to Wren and they lit up. After a couple of pulls on his beer, Wren propped his heels up on an empty crate and exhaled contentedly.

'You've done all right for yourself, Jacko. Landed on your feet by the look of it.'

Bass spat out a fragment of tobacco and drank some beer.

'It's not as good as it looks,' he said reflectively.

Wren grinned.

'You always did look on the bright side, Jacko. I still can't believe you joined up. Moment of madness was it; trying to impress some tart?'

Bass looked at Wren in surprise.

'The same reason as you, Charlie. We'd heard they'd got you. Then about two months later, I was up for affray – me of all people! With my record it would have meant two penn'orth at least. But with the war coming all the beaks were giving you the choice: sentence reserved for fourteen days and report to the Clerk of the Court. The clerk tells you, quietly like, that you'll really cop for it this time, but if you answer your Country's call and enlist, the case will be dismissed. Well, with everybody else volunteering, I thought: "Why not? A bit of the outdoor life, foreign travel, a uniform

46

and all the skirt after you; it's got to be better than porridge." What a mug I was! What I really copped for was five years living in mud and shit. That's if I'm lucky. I'm just as likely to get my bollocks blown off or a bullet in the guts.'

Wren nodded thoughtfully.

'That's right. Old Ted Bates came in on the same ticket as us. Remember Teddy? Worked for the Eagle brothers in Bermondsey. He made the same choice and was blown to bloody bits at Loos. I saw it.'

'There you are then, Charlie. You're not as smart as you think.'

'No,' Wren agreed, 'I'm not smart. But I don't live in mud and shit and I haven't been blown to bits – yet.' He reached for the beer bottle and replenished his glass. 'And you haven't done too badly either by the look of it, Jacko. You're living in clover as a gentleman's gentleman.'

'It's not clover being a slave to Mad Dog bloody Lovell,' Bass replied indignantly. 'That's what I am: a slave! He's a tyrant. I can't do anything without his say-so. I can't go to town. I get no leave. I'm stuck here all day every day. Cleaning his kit. Shining his boots. The only time I get out is on one of his stupid bloody errands.'

'You live well,' Wren pointed out, nodding at the stack of crates and provisions.

Bass glared unseeingly at the supplies, his resentment focused elsewhere.

'He's nasty, too, Charlie. Sadistic. He's always pushing me around. Trips me up when I'm carrying things. Punches me on the arm. Stupid things a school kid might do.'

Wren laughed involuntarily and Bass rounded on him.

'It's not funny, Charlie! He hasn't got the right to do things like that!'

'Get a transfer then,' Wren said. 'If you don't like it, transfer out.'

'He won't let me,' Bass replied intensely. 'I mentioned it

47

once, casually, to see how he'd take it. I told him I didn't think I was cut out to be a batman and he'd be better off with someone else.'

'What did he say?' Wren asked.

'He just laughed. He said: "Don't be silly, Jacko. You belong to me now, and you'd better get used to the idea." Then he said something that really scared me. I was putting some stuff away that he'd had sent out by Fortnum's: tins of ham, fruit, jam – that sort of thing – and he said: "Jacko, are you right-handed or left-handed?" and I said "Right-handed, sir". He said: "Let's have a look at your right hand then". And when I held it out he said: "Jacko, if you ever steal anything from me, I'll cut that hand off, and that's a promise." He tapped that bloody knife of his as he said it. And he meant it, Charlie!' Bass glared frantically at Charlie Wren. 'I know he meant it! Why would he say a thing like that, Charlie? Why?'

'Perhaps he doesn't like people nicking his stuff,' Wren said dryly.

Bass shook his head.

'There's more to it than that,' he said, lighting another cigarette with hands that were shaking slightly. He peered at Wren through the smoke. 'It was as if he knew about me. About my record. And yet I don't see how he could. Nobody in this company knows me. They're all north-country men. I was transferred in for no reason that I know of. I was clerking in the orderly room and Lovell happened to notice me. He had a few words, asked me where I came from – the usual bollocks. I thought he was just saying what officers always say. The next thing I know, he takes me on as his batman. It scares me, Charlie. I can sense that he's got it in for me but I don't know why. I can't think why it could be.'

The little man was clearly rattled and Wren sought to calm him.

'You're imagining things,' he said soothingly. 'He could

48

see you were good with figures and such like. He wanted somebody who could look at a bill and check it with the goods received – that sort of thing. Don't forget most of these Blaney men are mill hands or miners. He wanted someone with a bit of an education.'

'Then why does he kick me about and make my life a bloody misery?' Bass demanded.

Wren shrugged.

'All these titled bastards are half-mad,' he said reasonably. 'It's the inbreeding.'

'Well, I won't take it forever, ' Bass said fervently.

Suddenly he jumped up and strode to a cot standing against one wall. From under the pillow he took an object wrapped loosely in an army handkerchief. Bass discarded the handkerchief and drew from its scabbard a large straight-bladed knife.

'What the hell is that?' Wren asked in astonishment.

'It's a Shakespear Knife,' Bass said with a hint of pride.

'A what?'

'A Shakespear Knife. A hunting knife. I got it in a pawnshop in Bethnal Green. The old boy there told me a bit about it. It was designed by Major Shakespear, an explorer in India. He designed his own knives and had them made by Wilkinsons.'

'Let's have a look,' Wren said and Jacko handed it over.

Wren examined the knife closely. Its checkered leather handle was concave in design and gave an unusually sure grip. The flat, double-edged blade was about eight inches long. Sure enough, the etching on the blade said: *Shakespear Knife – Wilkinson London.*

'You could do someone a mischief with that,' Wren admonished, handing the weapon back.

Bass nodded fervently. 'That's the truth,' he said. 'And if Mad Dog bloody Lovell pushes me too far I'll do *him* with it.'

Wren laughed at the little man's passionate resolve.

'Takes more than a good knife, Jacko,' he goaded. 'Takes a good man behind it.'

Bass became even more incensed. He shook the blade of the knife in Wren's face and his voice rose to a shout.

'That's a promise, Charlie! I'm telling you! If that bastard ever hurts me again, he's going to get this – straight in the guts!'

4

Captain Lovell's team finally met in Mailly Maillet, a village two miles from the front. The village had provided billets and served as a headquarters base ever since the French army had handed it over to the British eleven months before. For the most part this had been a quiet sector and the village was still recognisable as such, but it had suffered intermittent attention from German artillery; many buildings had been damaged and, in the language of the troops, it was 'generally knocked about'.

There were five of them at the meeting: Captain Lovell, Hawker, Wren, Jacko Bass and Captain Grant of the Blaney Pals battalion which occupied the line in front of Serre.

Introductions were cordial but guarded. Lovell was keen to assess the men Sir John Trent had allocated him and Hawker and Wren were unsure how to treat someone of Captain Lovell's reputation. At first, Hawker was in awe of his hero but Lovell was gushingly polite and declared himself a great admirer of 'the intrepid bird-men' of the Flying Corps.

Wren and Bass greeted each other cursorily, as strangers. At their recent meeting in Lovell's billet they had decided that it would be better if their previous acquaintance was not generally known. They had, however, agreed on a secret alliance.

It had been Jacko's idea. After the second bottle of beer

he had begun to relax. When he learned they would both be accompanying Lovell on a raid, he threw Wren another cigarette and looked at him seriously.

'We should look out for each other, Charlie,' he said. 'We've got a lot in common.'

'Like what?' Wren said.

Bass thought for a moment.

'Well, we're not *old* army men out for promotion; and we're not *new* army men in for the glory. We stumbled into this lot by accident. If we stick together we might come out of it in one piece.'

Wren laughed ironically.

'You going to look after me, Jacko?'

'All right,' Bass admitted sheepishly, 'you can look after yourself, Charlie, we all know that. But it won't hurt any for you to know you've got someone on your side. Two heads are better than one. And I *know* Lovell; you don't. I can read him better than you. If he's up to something funny, I'll be able to warn you.'

'Why should he be up to something funny?' Wren said. Then he had a sudden thought. 'Has Lovell told you why we're going on this caper?'

'He hasn't told me much.' Jacko shrugged. 'He gave me some bullshit about going after buried treasure. Is that what you heard?'

'Something like that,' Wren said carefully. Then he grinned. 'D'you think there's any chance of us getting our sticky fingers on some loot?'

'Not a cat's chance in hell!' Bass said emphatically. 'Don't pull anything like that, Charlie, not with Lovell. Or if you do, leave me out of it. I don't want anything to do with it!' Bass had shaken his head thoughtfully. 'I don't even know why he's taking me along. Raiding's not my game. I'll only be in the way. I told him so.'

'What did he say,' Wren said.

'He said: "Don't be silly, Jacko. I need you to look after me." Then he laughed, nasty-like.'

Wren had to admit that it seemed odd bringing someone like Jacko along on a job like this. It didn't make sense. But then, in the army nothing made sense. The job they were about to do didn't make sense, but they would still do it. It didn't make sense to let characters like Lovell and Hawker run around loose, but loose they were.

'All officers are head-cases,' Wren said finally. 'You won't change that.'

And yet when he finally met Lovell, Wren was pleasantly surprised. After Sir John's description, Wren half expected someone in a white pith helmet and red tunic, but Lovell wore the regulation officers' Bedford cord breeches, khaki tunic and Sam Browne belt. The face above the tunic had kept its deep tan and the eyes above a strong nose and mouth were very pale blue. When he smiled – which was often – he displayed a fine set of even white teeth below a fair, close-clipped moustache. He moved quickly and confidently with an immense stride. *He'll be a bastard with women*, Wren thought enviously, but apart from his good looks there seemed nothing much to dislike about Captain Lord Rupert Lovell. His confidence was real and he had great charm. Unlike many officers, there was no arrogance about him. His manner was purposeful and direct but when he spoke to you it was with an interest and humour that was – or seemed – genuine.

There was nothing regular about his side-arms, two of which were carried on his belt to the left, for easy use with his right hand. The first of these was a big revolver carried well forward – almost on his belly – for an easy draw. Unusually for an officer, its holster had no flap and the pistol was held in place by a single strap across the hammer. On his hip, in a leather scabbard, lay what was either a short sword or long, broad-bladed knife. This, thought

Wren, must be the famous Khyber Knife. In addition, Lovell carried a short-barrelled Webley Mark 4 in a holster beneath his right armpit and two Mills Bombs hung by their split-pins on his belt.

After two years of war, Lovell was the first officer Wren had met who dressed as if he meant business. He was impressed but had no intention of showing it.

'Expecting trouble, sir?' he asked drily.

Lovell ignored the irony.

'I always expect trouble, sergeant,' he replied briskly. 'And trouble always expects me. We meet frequently!' He cast his eyes over the other's equipment and immediately noticed the shotgun. 'Hello, hello!' he remarked, 'what have we here?' He picked up the gun, sighted it at the ceiling and worked the lever action. 'Very *nice*, sergeant.' He looked at Wren with approval. 'Where did you get this?'

'I don't remember, sir,' Wren replied woodenly.

Lovell chuckled.

'Don't worry, I admire your initiative.' He drew his big pistol. 'I can see you're a connoisseur. What d'you think of this?'

'Webley isn't it, sir? Wren said puzzled.

Practically every officer in the British army wore a Webley revolver.

Lovell nodded and smiled.

'With a difference.' He weighed the pistol on the flat of his hand. 'Webley-Fosbery automatic revolver,' he said crisply. 'Chambered in .455. Single-action; quick-firing; very, very accurate.'

Wren had heard of the Fosbery. An unusual weapon, it had the appearance of a standard Webley but the frame of the pistol was split horizontally, so that the upper half holding the barrel and cylinder moved on a slide above the bottom half – the handle and trigger mechanism. For the first shot, the hammer had to be cocked with the thumb, but when the weapon was fired, the recoil threw the upper assembly back on its slide, turning the cylinder and cocking the hammer for the next shot. Because it was single action – a short trigger pull – and because the slide absorbed recoil, the pistol had great accuracy. Lovell gripped the pistol and profiled, extending his arm like a fencer.

'Standard Fosbery,' he said over his shoulder. 'But with wooden target grips and an extra two inches on the barrel. An extra two inches makes all the difference.'

'Yes, sir,' Wren replied. 'We'd all like an extra two inches.'

Lovell chuckled.

'I won this pistol at Bisley in 1911. It was first prize in a special competition run for Webley. The entrance fee was two bob and I won it with a best possible score. It's the best fighting pistol in the world. Also,' he added archly, 'because it's single-action, you can do this.'

Lovell crouched theatrically and spun the pistol cowboy-like on his forefinger. He spun it backwards, then forward, then backwards again and returned it to the holster with a flourish. He laughed aloud at his own proficiency.

Wren smiled faintly.

'I like the German automatics, sir.'

Lovell shrugged and made a face.

'They're cleverly made and they look pretty, but like all Hun stuff they're overengineered. The Germans are obsessed with perfection. It'll be their undoing in the end. You don't need a work of art to kill a man. Just a reliable tool.' He pulled the snub-nosed Webley from beneath his right armpit; it was a blunt, ugly thing. 'Up close, something like this'll do the job.' He nodded at Wren's shotgun. 'Or something like that. With the Fosbery for more refined work.'

Wren grinned.

'If you say so, sir.'

Lovell nodded emphatically.

'I do, sergeant, I do. And, hopefully, in time, I'll prove it to you.'

5

'That's Serre village on the right. Puisieux is on the left, further back.'

In a covered observation post behind the front line, Captain Grant, commander of 'A' Company, 1st Battalion Blaney Pals, pulled the sacking curtain carefully aside and pointed towards the enemy positions. Beside him, Philip Hawker and Captain Lovell squinted intently through their binoculars. Even as they watched, more shells were falling on Serre, raising smoke and dust. Over the past two years the village had been blown out of existence. First the French had pounded it to ruin, then the British had blasted it flat. Now it was a just-discernible blot on a devastated landscape.

Captain Grant had brought them up to show them the ground and explain how they were to penetrate the German line. Their vantage point was on raised ground behind the British line about a mile north of Auchonvillers. It looked straight across at the section of front line occupied by the Pals, the German position at Serre and the stretch of no man's land in between. The Pals' position lay in what was formerly a wooded valley, but the once lush forestry had been reduced to a chaos of blasted trunks and shell-pocked ground. Even so, the valley was out of direct view of the German lines and the smashed tree trunks gave a semblance of cover from enemy fire.

The 'wood' was made up of a line of four copses which

the British had named after the four apostles. From south to north, they were Matthew, Mark, Luke and John. John copse also marked the most northerly point of the planned British attack. In the event of a breakthrough, the whole of the British army in France would pivot left on Serre and begin a general advance north. From where they stood, the area had the appearance of an open book; with the wooded valley in the spine and the ground rising on both sides; sharply at first and then gently levelling as it stretched away to the British support trenches in the west, and eastwards towards the German front line at Serre.

'The German dugout I mentioned is on the far left on a line with Puisieux,' Grant went on. 'Originally, it formed a slight salient before it was battered and buried by our artillery and the Huns abandoned it and took the opportunity to straighten their line. Then recent shelling uncovered it again. The smashed bit sticks out into no man's land and a tunnel goes through into the Hun trenches. There's some timber guarding the exit – just to show that it's disused, I expect. But that can be pushed away easily enough.'

Knowing that the Blaney Pals was to be one of the first units 'over the top', Captain Lovell had shamelessly used his family's influence to get himself and his team attached to the battalion in the days leading up to the big attack. An 'A' Company night patrol had discovered the abandoned dugout a week ago and, after learning of Lovell's need to penetrate the German line prior to the attack, Captain Grant had generously offered it as a possible answer to the problem.

Grant's company would mount their usual patrol the night before the attack – this was to check the ground on their section of front and ensure that any new Hun wire had been cut. Lovell's team would accompany the patrol, which would guide them to the abandoned dugout. Once the group was ensconced in the dugout, the patrol would bomb the German line as a diversion then retire in the usual way. Lovell's men would spend the night in the dugout, sit out the artillery barrage which would precede the attack, and emerge as soon as the attack began. Moving behind the barrage as it switched to the rear areas, they would make their way to the next village, Puisieux, and thence across country to Flers.

Grant laughed suddenly.

'My Sergeant Tyke wanted to take a platoon and lie up overnight in the dugout with you chaps. He reckoned it would give them a good start on the Huns in the morning. But I had to forbid that, I'm afraid.'

'Why?' Lovell demanded.

'We can't have anything complicated like that,' Grant said, smiling and shaking his head. 'We must keep to the rigid timetable laid down by the artillery men. Everyone must know what everyone else is doing at any given time. The powers that be have come down very hard on any local innovations. Besides, if too many of you occupy the dugout, the Huns might rumble it and I don't want that. When we do go over we'll be making a beeline for it. It'll be our doorway into the German trenches.'

Grant suddenly punched the fist of one gloved hand into the other excitedly.

'By Golly!' he said, 'I can't wait to get on with it. It's going to be the most amazing success. I can't help feeling that you should be the one leading us, sir.'

Grant had been unable to forget their equal rank and felt compelled to defer to Lovell's family status.

'Mmm,' Lovell said distantly. He continued to scrutinise the enemy lines. 'I'm afraid Mr Hawker and I have other fish to fry.'

'Doesn't look very healthy over there does it, sir?' Hawker said brightly.

'We're not going for the benefit of our health,' Lovell retorted.

Hawker chuckled appreciatively.

'The attack will start at Oh-Seven-Thirty,' Grant said. 'When you hear the Hawthorn mine go up, that'll be your signal to get moving.'

'The Hawthorn mine?' Hawker queried.

'Yes. Two miles south of here, our people intend to explode a mine under the Hawthorn Redoubt – a German stronghold. A massive affair, twenty tons of explosive. When we hear that, we all get moving. And of course,' he added pointedly, 'when the Huns hear it, they'll know the attack has started.'

In an identical 'hide' twenty yards down the trench, Charlie Wren was also watching the torrent of shells raining down on Serre. He stared through the binoculars and snorted ironically.

'Looks like we're giving 'em a good kickin',' he said.

'I bloody hope we are!' Sergeant Tyke of the Blaney Pals replied fervently. 'One of these fine mornings, I'm going to have to take a walk over there.'

Wren watched the village for a moment longer then let the binoculars wander across no man's land to the British line. He reckoned it was about 300 yards from the blasted copses to the German front line and another 900 yards to the village. An infantryman, standing on the edge of the copses on a hot morning and looking up the slope towards Serre, would think it was a long way to walk carrying a bayoneted rifle and 60 pounds of equipment. But a battalion commander viewing it from here wouldn't consider it nearly so far. And to the general, finding it on his trench map, it would look no distance at all. Wren was glad he wouldn't be making the walk.

'And the best of luck!' he said finally.

He stepped down and seated himself beside Tyke on a makeshift seat excavated in the trench wall. Taking out his cigarettes, he gave one to Tyke and himself. He held a match for them both and the Pals man grunted his thanks, pulled his face away and exhaled contentedly.

'Pardon me for asking, Sergeant,' he said shyly, 'but you're *Charlie* Wren aren't you?'

Wren spat a fragment of tobacco.

'That's right,' he said guardedly.

The other grinned and extended his hand.

'Bob Tyke. Good to see you again, Charlie. You won't remember me but we met briefly in Boulogne in August '14, when we first got to France. You were a fusilier then and I was with the King's Own. You helped us out when there was a ruckus in that bar and the MPs came in mob-handed.'

Wren remembered it vaguely.

'That place on the waterfront?'

Tyke laughed happily.

'That's it. One of the barmaids was a fellah.'

Wren nodded and smiled at the memory. 'Yeh, she was quite tasty, too – apart from the Adam's apple.'

'You won't believe this, Charlie,' Tyke said grinning, 'but before the ruckus started, I went out the back for a run-out and saw our Regimental Sergeant Major with that barmaid. He had her stuck up against the wall. And to this day I don't know if the RSM knew that *she* was a *he*!'

'He probably knew,' Wren said. 'RSMs are funny people,' and they both laughed immoderately.

'So if you were in the King's Own, what are you doing in this Pals battalion?' Wren said conversationally.

Tyke shrugged.

'I got a bit of shrapnel at Neuve Chapelle. It was only a scratch but it went funny and they sent me back to Blighty

61

to get it fixed. I was a corporal then. When I was fit again they needed regulars to train up the Pals and offered me another stripe. I've no regrets. They're green but they're good lads.'

'I was at Neuve Chapelle,' Wren said, '*and* Wipers, *and* Loos. I'm an airman now – or thought I was.'

'You'll never get me up in one of them things,' Tyke said fervently. 'I like my feet on the ground!'

'Flying's all right,' Wren said. 'At least you see the sun every day.' He nodded his head towards the German lines. 'So when this show starts, what d'you think our chances are?' Wren asked.

Tyke nodded optimistically.

'I reckon they're good. The brass say it'll be a walk-over.'

Wren laughed shortly.

'We've heard that before.'

'I know,' Tyke said cynically. 'They've said it about every bloody attack we've ever made. But I reckon that this time they might be right. Be honest, Charlie, we've never seen planning and preparation like this.'

Wren nodded reluctantly.

'That's true.'

Tyke started counting points off on his fingers.

'Take training. We've got an area at the back made up and taped off exactly like the Serre defences. We've attacked it time and time again. We could do it blindfolded.'

'How many Huns have you got there?' Wren asked dryly.

Tyke ignored him.

'Take planning. We're all in on the plan. Every man knows where he's supposed to be at any given time throughout the attack.

'Communications: signallers with telephones and Morse buzzers will go over in the first waves so that the artillery

62

knows exactly where we are. We'll all be wearing tin triangles tied to the backs of our packs. Even if the signalling lines are cut, the tin will reflect the sun and the Flying Corps will be able to spot how far we've got.'

'They'll make prime targets if you have to run back,' Wren cracked.

'Artillery support. There's never been a barrage like this one, Charlie. It's been going on for days. And we've been clever with it. For a few days it lifts at the same time every morning. Then it'll suddenly stop a few minutes early, so that the Huns think we're coming. They start coming up out of their holes and then another bloody great barrage falls. It keeps 'em on the hop. Their nerves must be in shreds. By the time we do go, any machine-gunners left in Serre will be mental cases.'

'Don't look for machine-guns in Serre,' Wren put in. 'They'll be each side and further back. Their rear areas have just as good a view as we have here.'

'Counter-attacks.' Tyke was still counting. 'In the past, Charlie, the blokes that got into the first line of Hun trenches weren't strong enough to resist the counter-attacks. This time we're going across all tooled up and ready. Each man will be carrying sixty pounds of equipment: rifle ammunition, extra pans for the Lewis gunners, bombs, plenty of water and rations, even pickets and barbed wire.'

'How can you run 300 yards uphill carrying full packs?' Wren said fervently. 'The first wave should leave their packs and get across quick. Once they've got in the Hun trenches and bombed them out, they can hand over to the second wave and go back for their packs.'

'But listen to this,' Tyke went on. 'We've even dug shallow saps half-way across no man's land. At the end of them are concealed pits for Stokes Mortars. When the main barrage

63

lifts, the mortars will plaster the Hun forward trenches – give us extra support. You've got to hand it to the brass, Charlie. They've thought of everything.'

'No they haven't,' Wren retorted. 'They've thought hard about everything they could think of. There's a difference.'

'All right,' Tyke allowed. 'But that's all you can ask of anybody. I'll tell you what, I'd rather be us than some Hun stuck over there in a hole in the ground with all that shit falling on him.'

Wren nodded grudgingly. He didn't want to put the damper on the other's optimism.

'I reckon you're right. I must be getting windy in my old age.'

Tyke laughed.

'We're all getting like that. Anyone with any sense! These new army lads are cocky now. Wait 'till they see what that bloody Alley-man can do.' He shrugged and spoke more soberly. 'There's no sense in worrying. If your number comes up there's nothing you can do about it. The same shell that gave me my Blighty one at Neuve Chapelle killed my sergeant outright. Sergeant Garrett, the best NCO I ever served under; he put me up for my first stripe. But it had his name on it and there wasn't a thing he could do. Whichever way it goes, I've no complaints,' he said philosophically. 'Anything worthwhile I've ever done has been in the army. And I've seen a bit of the world.' Tyke brightened again suddenly. 'When I joined the Pals, our first posting was to Egypt. Where d'you think I spent last New Year's Eve, Charlie?'

Wren shook his head.

'Dunno.'

'On top of a pyramid!' Tyke said triumphantly.

Wren snorted with amusement.

'I hope there was a bar up there,' he said.

'Oh there was,' Tyke replied. 'We took it with us!'

They threw away their cigarettes and stood up expectantly at the sound of voices approaching along the trench. Captain Grant duly appeared followed by Lovell and Hawker.

'Well, Sergeant, ' Lovell said, addressing Wren breezily, 'now you've viewed the ground, what d'you think of the plan?'

'It's the best plan I've ever heard sir,' Wren replied straight-faced. 'I'm looking forward to it no end. The whole thing should be a piece of cake.'

Lovell looked at him in surprise for a moment. Then he laughed at some length and everyone except Wren joined in.

Half an hour later they were passing along a communication trench towards the Blaney Pals' forward positions opposite Serre. The sky was overcast and it had started to drizzle. The light was failing prematurely; there was no local shelling and it was unnaturally quiet. As they rounded a bend in the trench, they were challenged by the hushed but urgent tones of a sentry.

'Stand!' the voice commanded. 'Who goes there?'

'Friends!', Bob Tyke who was in the lead answered formally. '"A" Company officers and sergeants approaching the command post.'

Sentries were apt to become jumpy in times of quiet and he was taking no chances.

'Stand, friends,' the sentry replied authoritatively. 'Stand and give the password.'

Tyke said nothing.

'What's the password, Sergeant?' Captain Lovell demanded.

Tyke frowned and looked at him hard for a moment.

'There isn't one, sir,' he replied slowly.

Lovell drew his big pistol.

'Just a moment, sir,' Tyke held up his hand. 'Sentry,' he called, 'this is Sergeant Tyke with a party of officers. There *is* no password. State your name and rank.'

Silence.

Tyke made to move forward.

There was the rattle of a rifle bolt. 'Stand or I fire!' the sentry ordered. Then: 'Complete the following passwords: Bramall – '

'Lane', Tyke replied disgustedly.

'Blackpool – ,' the sentry prompted

'Rock,' Tyke shouted savagely. He peered into the gloom. 'Is that you, Meek?' he said suspiciously.

'Piccadilly – .'

'Private Meek, this is Sergeant Tyke,' Tyke shouted. 'I'm coming forward. If you shoot me I'll kick your arse from here to breakfast time!'

'Advance friend and be recognised,' the voice said hurriedly.

Tyke disappeared around the bend in the trench and there followed a dreadful fusillade of oaths. Lovell led the others forward and they found Tyke confronting the sheepish sentry.

Tyke was livid.

'What was all that bloody nonsense?' he demanded. 'You know my voice. You knew it was me.'

'Oh, I knew it was *you*, Sarge,' the sentry replied brightly. 'But the Huns could have snatched you in a raid. They might have been holding an automatic to your head, making you say those things.'

'I'll hold an automatic to *your* bloody head if you don't pipe down,' Tyke raged. 'You're on a charge. Report to me when you're relieved!'

'I was only being careful, Sarge,' Meek protested. 'Some funny things have . . .'

'Shut up!' Tyke bellowed. 'I'll deal with you later!' He

turned to Lovell apologetically. 'I'm very sorry about that, sir. Would you follow me now.'

Tyke led the way along the trench towards the Company CP. He was feeling unreasonably humiliated by the episode with the sentry and this was compounded by Lovell's stony attitude.

'I hope you'll be suitably severe with that man, Sergeant,' Lovell said at last. 'He was being deliberately insolent in front of officers.'

'I know what you mean, sir,' Tyke replied politely. 'And with any other man you'd be right. But Meek wasn't taking liberties, he was being serious. He's not quite the ticket, if you know what I mean, sir.'

'Tuppence short of a bob,' Hawker said laughing.

'I thought Private Meek was a good man, Sergeant,' Captain Grant put in, concerned that the whole episode was reflecting badly on his company.

'He's very keen, sir,' Tyke assented. 'But not quite all there.'

'Then he shouldn't be in the army,' Lovell retorted.

'I'm not so sure, sir,' Hawker quipped, artlessly putting into words what they were all thinking. 'Perhaps it's the best place for him!'

6

It was pitch dark in the dugout. Captain Lovell shone his torch on his wristwatch.

'One o'clock,' he said. 'We've got six hours to wait. We'll eat first and then try to get some sleep. Jacko, get that lamp lit and break out the goodies!'

Sergeant Tyke's three-man patrol had got them to their destination right on time. One of the mortar saps under no man's land had taken them almost to the enemy wire, then Tyke's practised route took them through the wire and up to the German line. Tyke showed them into the abandoned dugout, then he and his men faded into the darkness. A short time later they heard muffled explosions as Tyke's party bombed the German front line trench, then a fierce uproar of rifle and machine-gun fire as the Huns retaliated. This continued for 20 minutes or so until British shells began to thump above their heads and Lovell's party guessed that at least some of Tyke's patrol had got back safely.

Jacko Bass cleared a space on the ground and began to unload his heavy pack. First he extracted a hurricane lamp, set it on the ground and lit it with a match; then he spread a small tablecloth and began laying out food and drink. Lovell, Hawker and Wren seated themselves on sandbags or various bits of fallen timber and Bass handed out the grub.

There were ox-tongue sandwiches with mustard pickle; chicken and ham pie; cheese and crackers; and an apple each for dessert. The drink was bottled Perrier water laced with Scotch whisky. It was a real feast and after the tension of crossing no man's land, their appetites were up and they tucked in with gusto.

'I say, sir,' Hawker exclaimed as he selected a sandwich, 'this is like picnicking in the caves in Cornwall!'

Lovell snorted disparagingly and looked about him.

'I don't recall any caves quite like this, Lieutenant.'

Wren thought a word of appreciation was called for.

'Good groceries, sir,' he said through a mouthful of pie.

'Thank you, Sergeant', Lovell replied. 'Chaps who campaign with me deserve the best.' He smiled condescendingly at Jacko. 'Even Private Bass has his uses. He makes an adequate pack mule. I expect you were wondering why I brought him along. Now you know.'

Lovell laughed quietly to himself.

Bass looked at Wren and shook his head perceptibly.

They munched contentedly. Despite the squalid surroundings, the good food gave a feeling of well-being. They all carried water and hard-tack, but this would be their last decent meal for 24 hours.

Beside them lay their haversacks, belts and webbing. They were lightly armed: Lovell had his big knife and pistols; Wren the shotgun. Jacko Bass wore a regulation Webley revolver and Hawker had brought along a brand new Webley and Scott automatic pistol – a present from his father. Lovell and Wren also carried a quantity of Mills Bombs in their packs and on their webbing.

They were dressed in standard uniform but in place of greatcoats they all had thigh-length, sleeveless leather jerkins and carried waterproof ponchos rolled on their packs. At present they wore service caps, but each carried in his haversack what Lovell had called their secret weapon – a

69

German 'coal-scuttle' helmet that would be donned when they emerged into the enemy trenches.

The food was finished. Lovell went around with the whisky bottle topping everyone up.

'This should help us get some sleep,' he said. Then he set down his own cup and went over to the broken entrance to the dugout, inspecting it carefully and placing some heavy pieces of timber across to ensure that they wouldn't be surprised by a German patrol. He tried the barricade with his boot.

'No one'll come through there,' he said decisively. 'I won't post a sentry,' he added, cocking his head at the distant rumble of artillery. 'The barrage'll wake us up.'

Watching him, Wren had to admit that Lovell led from the front. He could give orders when necessary, but generally he got on with things, willing others to match his energy and pace. His dynamic leadership inspired confidence; for the first time since hearing about this job, Wren really felt they could see it through.

They finished the drink and, using their packs as pillows, stretched out on the hard, uneven ground. Above their heads shells rumbled lazily, alternately advancing and receding. Gradually, as the whisky took hold, they all drifted into sleep.

It was a restless night. After a couple of hours drink-induced sleep they were constantly disturbed by shells falling close by or by the sleepless sounds of their companions. They lay as quietly as possible, feigning sleep and trying to doze. But at 6.30 a.m. even this pretence became impossible. In a matter of seconds, the barrage above their heads rose to a terrific, vibrating roar as every British gun concentrated on the German front line. Everyone sat up and Jacko lit the lamp again. Previously, Lovell had forbidden smoking in case a passing Hun patrol smelt the smoke; but now he gave permission and everyone except Hawker lit up. They sat there, smoking and trying to relax, listening to the shells bumping above and trying to ignore the steady trickle of dislodged earth falling from the trembling beams in the dugout roof.

Lovell consulted his watch.

'Oh-Seven-Hundred,' he said. 'Thirty minutes to go.'

They fastened their webbing, gathered their packs and put on the German helmets. It was a tense moment but the donning of the huge helmets prompted an outbreak of wry humour.

'This,' said Lovell grimly, tightening the chin strap of his own dome, 'is a prime example of Hun overengineering.'

'I don't know, sir,' Hawker laughed. 'I could camp out under this!'

The neck-guard of his helmet almost rested on his shoulders.

'Better than a brolly if it rains, sir,' Wren said. He nodded ironically at Jacko Bass. 'This'll test your neck muscles, Jacko.'

'This thing weighs a ton!' Bass complained.

'Without these,' Lovell reminded them, 'we'd have no chance of passing unnoticed behind enemy lines. You'd better get used to them.'

Lovell and Wren cleared the timber barring the exit. Jacko dowsed the lamp, wrapped it in a cloth and stowed it in his pack. It was 7.15 a.m. They crouched in the darkness, steeling themselves for the last quarter of an hour. Then a few minutes later the noise of shells was drowned by the rumble of a greater, more distant explosion. The sound and concussion rolled towards them deep underground and the earth all around shook violently.

'That's the mine at Hawthorn!' Lovell said in surprise. He snapped on his torch and looked at his watch. 'It's only twenty past. They're ten minutes early!'

His voice and his face in the yellow torchlight registered concern. And the others, crouching in the dark, knew what he was thinking. The attack was due to start at 7.30 a.m. At precisely that time, all along the 18-mile front, extended lines of British soldiers would climb out of their trenches and move towards the German lines. If any German defenders were left alive in their pounded dugouts, the sound of the exploding mine would tell them the attack had started. They then had to get their riflemen and machine-gunners up the dugout steps and into the front-line trenches before the attacking British reached them. If the entire attack had been brought forward ten minutes, no harm would be done. But if the time of the attack was unchanged and the Hawthorn mine had gone up prematurely, then the German defenders would have a ten-minute start. Ten minutes would be plenty of time for them to accomplish a task they had been rehearsing for eleven months.

But as the shock of the Hawthorn explosion rolled away northwards the shelling too ceased.

'I hope they know what they're doing,' Lovell said finally. 'We'd better get moving.'

They shouldered packs and followed the captain up the stairs into the daylight. The air up above was thick with dust and the acrid stink of high explosive. They moved quickly along their planned route, following the wrecked trench system towards Puisieux. The barrage had cleared their way and had now lifted to fall onto the second line of defences. In a while they would go to ground again and wait until it cleared to the third. They kept straight ahead, resisting the urge to look back.

Behind them, German machine-gunners emerged from their dugouts deep in the chalk. They had plenty of time to choose their vantage points and set up their precision weapons. The morning was bright and clear. With the risen sun at their backs, the Germans watched and waited. At exactly 7.30 a.m. the attacking elements of the British army – Kitchener's new, volunteer army – climbed out of their trenches and began to advance.

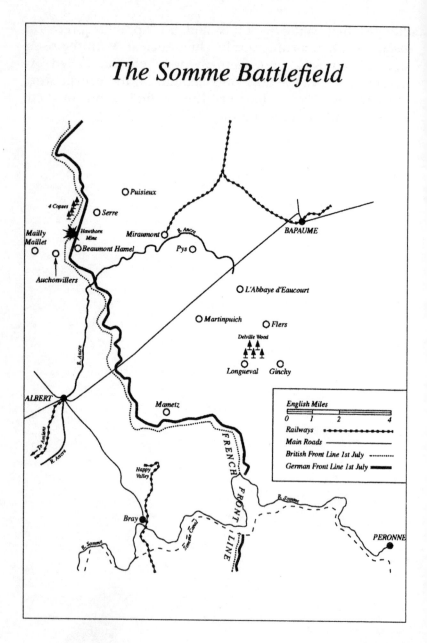

The Somme Battlefield

O Puisieux

4 Copses
O Serre

Mailly
Maillet
O

Hawthorn
Mine
O Beaumont Hamel
Miraumont O
R. Ancre
Pys O

Auchonvillers

BAPAUME

O L'Abbaye d'Eaucourt

O Martinpuich
O Flers

Delville Wood

Longueval   Ginchy

R. Ancre

ALBERT

O Mametz

To Amiens

R. Ancre

FRENCH

FRONT

Happy
Valley

R. Somme

LINE

R. Somme

PERONNE

Bray

Somme Canal

English Miles

| 0 | 1 | 2 | 4 |

Railways ••••••••••••••••
Main Roads ———————
British Front Line 1st July ·············
German Front Line 1st July ▬▬▬▬

7

Captain Grant, of 'A' company, 1st Battalion Blaney Pals, was worried. Five minutes before, he had got his company out of the front line trench and had them lie down on the edge of no man's land. Now he lay in the long grass alongside the forward platoon and debated with himself what to do. His orders were clear. At zero hour he was to advance behind the barrage and occupy the enemy's front-line trenches, secure them and prepare to receive counter-attacks. The supporting company would then pass through and attack the enemy's second line.

Zero hour was 07.30 hours, but the mine under the Hawthorn Redoubt had been detonated ten minutes early. At the same time, the barrage that had been pounding the German line for seven days and nights had suddenly ceased. There had been no answering barrage from the enemy. No rattle of machine-guns. Nothing but an eerie silence enhanced by the cheerful sound of birds: skylarks calling; a blackbird's diligent phrase; the petulant shouts of sparrows.

Already the sun was a hand's-breadth above the horizon and strong enough to hurt the eyes. The captain looked at his watch. Still five minutes to go. If they went too early and the barrage started up again they would be right under-neath it.

Grant came from an old family of Blaney mill owners. When war broke out and Blaney's weavers and cutters rushed to answer Kitchener's call, Grant had considered it his duty to go with them. Their first posting was to Egypt where they had hardened their identity as a unit, confirmed their supremacy as Englishmen in an inferior world and seen real sunshine for the first time in their lives. But now it was time for the test. This was the 'Big Push' that would knock the Hun for six out of France and Belgium. All the months of planning, organisation and effort had come to this: a silent moment in time. Kitchener's army waited on the brink and the Empire held its breath.

But Grant still hesitated and his caution was shared by assault commanders all along the front. The Hawthorn mine had gone up and the Germans now knew the attack was starting. But zero hour was 7.30 a.m. and the orders were clear. Grant could sense the tension building up behind him. The overcrowded support trenches would be choked with heavily-laden men, pressing forward, cursing and jostling for space. Grant remembered the line from Macaulay: *Those behind cried 'Forward'; and those before cried 'Back!'* and even in his present state he could see the humour of it. He laughed suddenly and the men around him stirred expectantly. He thought: *I'll have to move now, or they'll think I've gone barmy.*

He looked at his watch. It was almost half past and there was still no sign of the barrage starting again. He stood up and looked around. Still silence. He could see the rows of men stretching along the length of the front, almost invisible in the long grass. The bright sun shone on their bayonets and on the silver triangles tied to their packs. He surveyed the distant, dust-shrouded ridge in front of him. Nothing moved there. There was no bark of a mortar, no chatter of a Maxim. He breathed deeply with relief. It was all right. The barrage had done its job. All the defenders were dead. It was going to be a walkover.

His head came up and he waved his walking stick and

called cheerily to the men, 'Come along then. Who's for a stroll before breakfast?' He laughed at their hesitation. 'Come along! Don't dawdle! I'll race . . .'

Grant stopped shouting as something struck him heavily in the throat. In the same instant the use went out of his legs and he fell helplessly on top of the man beside him. He tried to shout an order but his throat was constricted by a massive rush of blood. In another moment he was dead.

When Grant stood up, Sergeant Bob Tyke had been lying beside him. As the captain called on them to rise, Tyke went onto one knee and balanced his pack. He was concentrating on transferring the weight carefully to both feet when Grant suddenly collapsed and fell on top of him, blood rushing from his open mouth. As Tyke struggled to disentangle himself from the weight of his dead officer, he looked along the line of his men. Some had been hit and lay still; others were crying out in pain. Those who were all right were watching him, waiting for him to tell them what to do. There came the sudden shriek of an incoming shell. Tyke placed his face flat against the earth and watched the shell explode 50 yards down the line. There were screams and shouts for stretcher-bearers.

More shells fell, all along the line. Tyke knew that he would have to stand up and lead the men forward. The Huns had them bracketed; if they stayed here they would be shelled to buggery. He wanted very much to stay where he was but you couldn't always do what you wanted, not when you had three stripes on your arm. And he felt the dull ache in his belly that you get when you know you have to do something you'd give anything *not* to do.

He pulled his tin hat low over his eyes and squinted at the distant ridge. There was no visible sign of the enemy. Far off to the left a Maxim gun was talking and to their immediate front there was a rush and commotion; a hazing of the air as the seeding grass was cut by a thousand tiny scythes. He hoped the machine-gun would pause for a moment and give them a chance, but it went on and on and was joined by another on the right. He thought that Charlie Wren had been right about the machine-guns; and about the packs. At least without their packs they would have had the comfort of running and the notion of a chance.

The motion in the grass moved back and forth like a wind. It seemed to wander away to his right and, on an impulse, he stood up. He looked left and right at the perfectly dressed line of men, lying prone in the grass and almost obscured by the bulks of their packs.

He waved his bayoneted rifle at them and shouted, 'Come on! Get moving! Get moving!'

It sounded like someone else's voice. He began to walk forward and slowly, hesitantly, all along the line men started to rise to their feet.

He walked on steadily. The grass was heavy with dew and last night's rain so that his boots and puttees were soon soaked through. More machine-guns were starting: to the left and right and now directly in front. Tyke knew he wouldn't get far; there was no chance at all. The Huns were ready and waiting. But he had no choice; the men's eyes were on him; better to be dead than fail now. He had never been a religious man but he prayed fervently that when it came it would be quick and clean. He walked steadily on, his lips moving in prayer; and to the watching men it appeared that he walked with disdain, mouthing curses at the enemy. And they pressed on, hurrying to keep up, determined not to let him or themselves down. All along the front men moved forward into increasing machine-gun and shellfire; to be cut down singly; and in groups; and in long, neat rows.

Bob Tyke had gone 200 yards now, more than half-way across no man's land, but the effort had been so great that he felt he must soon lie down and rest. He was suddenly startled by a small explosion on his right, but it was only one of the Stokes mortars firing from its hidden pit. Tyke took some comfort from this but seconds later it fired again, and in the same instant a machine-gun bullet struck him in the head. As he fell, Tyke was convinced he had been killed by a mortar bomb falling short.

Private Michael Meek was five paces behind when Bob Tyke fell shot in the head. Meek knelt briefly beside the body but the sergeant lay quite still and his face was a mask of blood. Meek had had many run ins with Tyke but he had immense regard for him as a man and a soldier and was consumed with hate for the Germans who had killed him. He wanted to riddle them with lead, rip at their bodies with his bayonet and tear them to pieces with his bare hands. A red mist rose before his eyes and he rushed blindly forward until he was brought up short by the enemy wire and fell in a heap, tearing his hands and clothes on the razor-sharp barbs.

Panting with exertion, he looked for a way through and at last found a gap where the shelling had done its work. A Maxim gun was firing close by and he took a Mills bomb from his side pocket and drew the split-pin. Carefully holding the lever in place, he looked about and found himself completely alone. The ground behind was littered with the fallen bodies of his comrades. Ahead was the enemy who had killed Sergeant Tyke and all of his mates. Meek wept with anger and grief. The Germans were cowards and scum; lower than vermin. They invaded defenceless countries and skulked behind machine-guns and barbed wire. The Blaney Pals had been decent lads who had come to seek justice and right. And now they were all dead. But there was still *one* Blaney man to teach the Huns a lesson.

Sniffing back his tears, Meek strode forward, passed through the wire and came upon the Maxim team changing the belt. He released the lever, held the bomb for a few seconds then lobbed it carefully at the gun. The Germans had a second to see the bomb before it exploded, killing three of them. Meek charged the other two, sinking his bayonet into a man's chest and crushing the other's skull with his rifle butt.

Meek dropped down into the front-line trench. Close by was a traverse and beyond it he could hear the sound of foreign voices. Peering round, he discerned a party of the enemy coming towards him. Smiling at the surprise he would cause, Meek pulled out his last bomb. He released the lever and tossed it over the traverse. When it exploded he rushed forward firing his rifle from the hip. As the nearest Huns turned to run, he jammed his bayonet up to the hilt in a man's back. He had his hands locked around another's throat when the Germans finally gathered themselves and clubbed and stabbed him to death.

When Private Meek died he had accounted for ten of the enemy single-handed. He was the only man of the Blaney Pals to reach the German front line. But his feat went unrecorded and his body was never found.

8

It was a mile to Puisieux and downhill all the way, but Lovell had expected it to be the most dangerous part of their journey. A small group of soldiers hurrying to the rear were liable to be stopped and questioned. From the debris of the wrecked trenches, Lovell soon acquired a large coil of telephone wire and a couple of long-handled shovels. His plan was for them to pose as field engineers looking for breaks in the telephone line. He hoped this might also allay any suspicion regarding their different dress and equipment.

In the forward area, the German telephone network followed the trench system, the wires themselves being neatly labelled and secured to the trench walls. If confronted by German infantry, Lovell's group would cut an adjacent wire and busy themselves 'repairing' it, hoping that the advancing Huns would be too anxious and preoccupied to heed them.

Yet strangely, on the way to Puisieux, they encountered no one. Once in the village they observed several large groups of infantry crouching in trenches at the roadside – reserves being held in readiness; but no one bothered them and they struck out thankfully on the road to Miraumont.

Now that they were now moving behind and parallel to the front, they were less likely to be challenged. But the going became harder and the road undulating. The main

British barrage travelled above their heads but occasional shells still sought and found the road. It was severely cratered in places and they were forced to skirt around, blundering into the surrounding trench system, becoming disorientated and wasting time finding the road again.

It was in the course of one of these diversions that they had their first serious encounter with the enemy. They were passing along a German communication trench which by-passed a wrecked stretch of road: Lovell leading; Hawker behind him; Bass and Wren bringing up the rear. It was hard going. The trench had been recently flooded and was slick with liquid mud. Going uphill they dug with their toes and clawed with bare hands at the rain-softened walls. Downhill they moved on their heels, bracing themselves for a fall and judging each step with frantic attention.

They slopped grimly along, making steady progress when, without warning, the ground disappeared beneath Jacko's feet and he found himself up to his armpits with his legs hanging terrifyingly in thin air. This was nothing unusual. The Western Front was made up of a hundred million holes in the ground. Every infantryman in France had fallen into something nasty at some time or other. It might be a breather hole to an ancient bunker or a shaft drilled by a dud shell; or the earth simply giving up under the weight of iron, water and human bodies pressing down on it. Nobody cared what caused it; your only concern was that someone was on hand to get you out.

Charlie Wren, following behind, went down on one knee and stuck his left arm under Jacko's armpit to stop him going further down. He called as loudly as he dared to Hawker and Lovell but they failed to hear and promptly disappeared around a bend in the trench. Wren still wasn't bothered. He shushed the cursing Bass into silence, unslung his shotgun and propped it carefully against the trench wall. Then he got Jacko's pack off, planted his legs firmly and heaved. Bass was a lightweight without his pack and Wren soon had him out, except at the last moment the little man clung and fell against him, rolling them both in the mud.

They were both peeved at this performance but it was everyday stuff and they cursed and helped each other back to a standing position. Wren had collected himself and was stooping to retrieve his gun, when he became aware that someone was rounding the corner of the trench where Hawker and Lovell were last seen. Wren assumed that one or both of them had returned and was already composing his features in an expression of ironic disgust. But instead of Hawker and Lovell, he came face-to-face with a three-man German work party.

The leading Hun carried a sack of provisions and a slung rifle while the other two manhandled a species of cooking pot – an outsized billy-can slung between them on a pole. When Wren first turned, the lead man had already discarded his sack and unslung his rifle. His companions remained astonished and rooted to the spot, still crouching with the cooking pot suspended between them. As Wren turned away and reached for his gun, he heard the rattle of the rifle bolt and knew he was going to be too late. When he turned back, the rifle was up and pointing. He was bracing himself for the bullet when the man's face exploded and he pitched forward into the mud. Behind him, at the corner of the trench, Captain Lovell stood with his right arm outstretched, the long-barrelled Fosbery smoking in his hand.

The two remaining Germans dropped their burden and started to run. One darted down an adjacent trench while the other long-jumped over his fallen comrade, rushed straight past Wren and around the next bend.

Lovell shouted, 'Your bird, sergeant!' then calmly shifted his stance through ninety degrees and fired twice after the first fleeing Hun.

Wren gripped the Winchester and went after his man. Around the corner they were in a straight stretch of trench. The Hun was ten yards ahead. Wren checked in his stride, tucked the stock of the shotgun into his armpit and fired. The man fell forward, a gaping hole across his spine.

Wren levered another round into the breech; he knew what had to be done. The man's legs were useless and he was trying to drag himself forward with his forearms. As Wren approached, he started to turn his head. Wren did it quickly, holding the gun close to the back of the skull. He turned away, levering the breech again and topping up the magazine with two fresh shells from his pocket.

Back at the scene, Lovell was reloading his pistol. He looked at Wren enquiringly. Wren just nodded.

'You were caught napping there, Sergeant,' Lovell admonished. 'I expected better of you.'

'Sorry, sir,' Wren said. He felt unreasonably guilty. 'We had a bit of trouble. Private Bass had fallen into a bloody great hole. We were just sorting it out when the Huns appeared.'

Lovell sneered down at Jacko, covered in liquid mud and miserably trying to compose himself.

'Private Bass can't seem to do right for doing wrong. He's a complete waste of space.'

Lovell turned away disdainfully.

'That's right,' Bass mumbled resentfully, 'blame me for everything!'

'You *are* to blame!' Wren shot at him.

He was still furious with himself for being caught out. For some reason he had found himself wanting to impress Captain Lovell, but had failed at the first opportunity.

'I didn't fall into that bloody hole on purpose, Charlie,' Bass said, looking hurt.

He expected blame from Lovell but Wren was supposed to be an ally.

84

'We're not on a bloody picnic.' Wren hissed. 'For Christ's sake look where you're going!'

'Any trouble, chaps?' Hawker asked brightly, appearing late on the scene.

Captain Lovell had turned back to look for the others leaving Hawker alone. Hawker had heard the shots and hurried back, his automatic pistol clutched determinedly in his hand.

'No trouble, Lieutenant,' Lovell grinned. 'You can dispense with the artillery.'

He slapped Hawker on the back and they turned and made their way back up the trench.

Still sneering at each other, Wren and Bass followed, turning their backs on three corpses and an upturned can of stew still steaming in the mud; all that remained of three men who went to fetch their breakfast down a flooded trench – and were killed for it.

9

Captain Lovell had his binoculars out, scrutinising the area around them.

'Horses,' he said to himself, loud enough for them all to hear. 'I'm looking for horses.'

''Orses?' Jacko Bass replied.

'Yes,' Lovell replied drily. 'You know, noble creatures with a leg at each corner. You can ride on their backs.'

'I can't ride an 'orse, sir,' Bass said fervently.

'Nor can I, sir,' Wren said quickly.

'I'm afraid I don't ride very well either, sir,' Hawker chimed in.

Lovell looked at them in wonder.

'But everyone can ride. It's just a question of getting on and making them go!'

They had no answer to that and Lovell pressed home his advantage.

'If we can find horses, we'll ride,' he asserted. 'It'll save time.'

They were lying away from the road close to the river on the eastern edge of Miraumont. Lovell had decided to rest for a while. They all drank some water and Jacko passed around bars of chocolate. The journey was proving harder than Lovell had anticipated. So far it had taken four hours but it wasn't so much the time that worried him as the physical state of his companions. Sergeant Wren was still

86

strong but Hawker and Bass were beginning to flag. They were not yet half way to Flers; and he had to admit that after another five or six hours' slog he'd be fit for nothing himself. He therefore began to consider some method of transport.

Miraumont lay in the valley of the River Ancre. The river was shallow here and only a few yards across but its steep-sided, snaking valley provided the Germans with valuable cover. The roads in and around the village were packed with motor wagons and infantry. Off the road, every clear space harboured a big gun. The British barrage had already moved on but the valley was thick with guns and howitzers, all untouched and firing furiously towards Auchonvillers and Serre.

Lovell didn't like the look of it. He had been surprised when they met no reinforcements on the way to Puisieux and had hoped it was because the Huns had been over-whelmed by the week-long barrage. But the fact that reserves were being held back indicated that they weren't needed, which gave him concern about the success and progress of the British attack.

'Horses,' Lovell repeated tauntingly. 'That's what I'm looking for.'

'What about an iron horse, sir?' Hawker asked tentatively.

'Iron horse?' Lovell said slowly and followed Hawker's eyes into the valley where the sun shone on metal and plumes of steam rose skywards. The rush and grind of heavy machinery could just be discerned above the crashes of artillery.

'Yes, sir,' Hawker smiled. 'The German army likes horses but what they really love is railways. Behind every German front line is a network of narrow-guage railways.'

'Is that so?' Lovell replied. 'And if we were able to get our hands on a locomotive, who's going to drive it.'

'Why, me, sir,' Hawker laughed. 'With you're permission, that is.'

Lovell looked at him and smiled faintly.

'Hawker, you bird-men never cease to amaze me. All right, I'll buy it. Let's find a steam engine!'

Bob Tyke was dreaming. He dreamt he was lying in his coffin in the little parlour at home, while his mother and sisters looked down at his disfigured corpse and wailed with grief. The wailing went on until it made his head ache. Finally, he came to and realised he was lying on the grass in no man's land, but the wailing continued and his head still ached.

He explored his face with a hand and found that his skin had been badly burnt by the sun; his lips were dry and cracking and there was a crusty, congealed hole where his right eye had been. Tyke moaned at the discovery and became miserably aware that the wails in his dream were the moans of other wounded men lying around him.

The sun was high in the sky and he felt around for his helmet. It was hot to the touch but he put it on and peered at his wristwatch with his good eye. It was nearly noon. He found his water bottle and took a good quantity of the warm, brackish water. He was thankful that his movements hadn't attracted the attention of Hun snipers and he began cautiously to explore the area.

The field was thick with dead and wounded. The wounded were calling for water and Tyke began to crawl carefully from body to body. From the dead he took more water bottles and carried them to the conscious wounded. Many of them were too far gone to help and if they were quiet he left them be. With some of the abler ones he had a few words, telling them to hold on until dark when they could have a go at crawling back to the start line.

In a shell hole he came upon three men. One had a terrible stomach wound and was almost comatose, but every few minutes he called in a bull-like voice for his mother. Another had lost both hands. He sat quite still, patiently explaining to himself; 'But I can't go home like this. I can't go back to Annie like this.'

The third was trembling and weeping uncontrollably. He had lost control of his bladder and urine mingled with the blood stagnating at the bottom of the hole.

Tyke found a comfortable shelf just below the lip of the crater. He placed his helmet over his face and waited for the day to end. It had been a bloody awful day but he was one of the lucky ones. He had lost an eye but still had sight and all his limbs and faculties. Under cover of darkness, he would start to crawl back to the British lines. If he could only get there, he would soon be home. In the valley beyond the copses, a narrow-gauge railway carried the wounded to the main railhead at Buire-sur-l'Ancre. A proper train would take him down to where the river became navigable and then he'd be transferred to one of the canal barges that went all the way through the Somme valley to the sea. The army would look after him.

Tyke relaxed and began to doze. The moans and cries around him diminished and he imagined himself already on the canal with the sights and sounds of the water; the warmth and smells of the grassy bank; the flutter and splash of river creatures scurrying away at the barge's approach. Soon even these left him and he slept deeply.

10

At last it was dark enough. With Captain Lovell in the lead, they crept from their hiding place among the piles of munitions into the shadow of the railway embankment. As they got closer they could make out the outline of the locomotive and hear the crunch of the sentry's boots on the shale between the tracks.

At midday, when Hawker had suggested stealing a locomotive, they had moved from their position near the river and gone in search of the railway line. But as they got closer it became clear that they had stumbled on a major rail depot.

The area was a hive of activity. Full and narrow-gauge engines shunted back and forth. Gangs of soldiers stripped to the waist laboured among the trucks, loading and unloading, passing heavy shells from hand to hand. Cranes swung overhead, lifting and shifting, piling up munitions and supplies.

Like the British south of Albert, here at Miraumont the Germans were still operating the old French standard-gauge railway. Supplies coming in on the main line from Bapaume and Arras were then transferred to a network of narrow-gauge tracks servicing front-line positions.

Lovell took out his map. He and Hawker watched the railway activity and studied the lie of the land. Narrow-gauge tracks ran in many directions but one clearly headed out along the valley towards the villages of Pys, l'Abbaye d'Eaucourt and Flers. If they could commandeer a train on this line, it would cut out the hours of footslogging and get them to Flers refreshed and ready for anything.

But with all this human activity, it would be impossible to get their hands on an engine in daylight. They would have to wait for dark. Lovell wasn't bothered by this. The rest would do them good and he had intended to lie low for a few hours once they had got to Flers. And the railway was safer; once they were aboard and moving, no one would challenge an engine and trucks.

Now it was 10.00 p.m. There was still some rail movement over on the main line, but here on the edge of the depot where the narrow-gauge track headed towards Flers, it was quiet. The labourers and railwaymen had dispersed, leaving an occasional bored sentry to walk his beat between avenues of piled munitions, cooling engines and dark, silent trucks.

They heard the crunch of shale on the track above and could just make out the sentry's silhouette as he wandered slowly away from them. Lovell drew the Khyber Knife. The 15-inch, double-edged blade gleamed darkly as he moved silently up the bank into the shadow of the engine. The others waited breathlessly. They heard the sentry turn and retrace his steps until he seemed to stop directly above their hiding place. He stamped his feet on the sleepers and rubbed his hands in an effort to get warm. There was the slightest of sounds followed by the thump of a falling body, and a dark football-like object rolled down the bank towards them.

'Catch that!' Lovell hissed urgently.

Jacko Bass dived and caught it with a game effort, only to hurl it away again with a strangled shriek of protest. Wren, crouching beside him, saw what it was. It was the sentry's severed head. Jacko shuddered and desperately scrubbed his hands on the grass.

'Barmy bastard,' he muttered resentfully and they heard Lovell's quiet laughter.

Quickly they scrambled up the bank and gathered beside the engine. Lovell was cleaning his knife with a handful of grass.

As the others came up he announced in a sing-song voice, 'The train standing at platform one is the non-stop service to Flers. All abo-a-r-d!' He chuckled softly and looked at Hawker. 'Time to do your stuff, Lieutenant.'

'Right sir,' Hawker replied. 'Come on, Charlie!'

The little tank engine was less than 20 feet long and was mounted on a chassis so low that there was only one step up from the track to the footplate. Its compact design and pleasing lines had Hawker chortling with pleasure.

'Just look at this little loco, Charlie,' he enthused swinging up into the tiny cabin. 'It's not only a marvellous machine; it's positively beautiful. You've got to hand it to the old Hun!'

He opened the firebox door and began shovelling coal from the side-bunker. The fire was still hot but the fresh coal was slow in catching. Charlie Wren took a paraffin lamp from the corner of the cab and threw it into the firebox.

'Good man!' Hawker exclaimed.

He smashed the lamp with his shovel and the fire leapt into life.

Hawker moved easily around the cabin, laying his hands on the controls; locating the regulator, reversing lever and steam brake.

'You see, Charlie,' he said contentedly, 'after the Franco-Prussian war, General Hellmuth von Moltke realised that nowadays the supply lines to a battle are more important than the battlefield itself. He said: "Don't build me fortresses; build me railways!" The Huns have got hundreds of these little chaps working behind the lines all over the Western Front.'

'Really, sir?' Wren replied dryly.

'Absolutely,' Hawker nodded vigorously. 'On a modern battlefield, munitions and men are expended so quickly that the army that can deliver an endless stream of supplies to the front is bound to prevail. Which is why *our* service, the Royal Flying Corps, is so important. Only the aeroplane is able to strike at roads and railway lines miles behind the front. Eventually,' Hawker explained, 'with bigger and better aeroplanes, it will make more sense to bomb German factories, thereby destroying guns and shells before they are even despatched to the front and, at the same time, destroying the enemy's capacity to replace them.'

'Wouldn't that mean killing civilians, sir?' Wren asked.

Hawker thought for a moment.

'Not necessarily. Precision bomb sights would have to be developed allowing us to bomb the factories while leaving dwellings untouched.'

'All this will probably take some time then, sir,' Wren suggested.

'Certainly, ' Hawker replied.

'So you think the war will go on for a long time yet, sir?'

'Absolutely,' Hawker said happily. 'I should think it'll go on for *years*.' He tapped the glass of the steam gauge impatiently. 'Come on Hellmuth!' he urged, addressing the engine.

Captain Lovell appeared and thrust his head into the cabin.

'How's it coming, Hawker? he demanded.

'Almost there, sir,' Hawker replied. 'We have to wait for steam-up.'

He tapped the steam gauge again and shovelled more coal into the firebox.

'This is all very impressive, Lieutenant!' Lovell said, smiling at Hawker's industry. 'I've disconnected the train after the first wagon. There's no sense in pulling that lot along with us.'

'Good show, sir,' Hawker said. 'That'll make it easier to drive.' He looked at the steam gauge again and knocked the firebox door shut with his shovel. He nodded to Lovell. 'That's it, sir. We can go.'

Hawker spun the wheel of the handbrake and released the steam brake. Jacko Bass, waiting morosely beside the engine, leapt in panic as a cloud of steam from the waste pipe enveloped him.

Lovell laughed delightedly.

'Move yourself, Jacko! he taunted. He stepped onto the footplate. 'Sergeant Wren, take private Bass and get aboard the first wagon. I'll ride with the driver.'

'Right, sir,' Wren said, jumping down.

He and Jacko went and climbed into the first box-wagon.

Hawker set the reversing lever and pulled the regulator gently towards him. The engine panted eagerly. The drive wheels skidded briefly, then gained full traction and steadily picked up speed.

'We can't go too fast, sir,' Hawker shouted. 'I don't know the track and I've had no practice with the brakes.'

His face was blackened from the coal and he wore his service cap reversed on his head. Grasping the steam regulator with his left hand, he leaned out of the right-hand doorway squinting into the dark turmoil of smoke and steam.

Lovell grinned at him.

'This is fine!' he shouted. 'So where did you learn to drive a steam locomotive, Lieutenant?'

'A friend of my father, sir,' Hawker replied. 'He built a narrow-gauge railway in the grounds of his estate. For two

94

weeks every summer, when his driver was on holiday, he let me run the railway.'

'He must be very wealthy,' Lovell said.

'He *is* wealthy,' Hawker admitted. 'But he claims the railway is very cost-effective. Besides going around the grounds, the track also runs to the nearest main-line station. He uses it to supply coal for domestic heating and power. He needs five thousand tons a year and he reckons the railway saves him fourpence a ton per mile.' Hawker laughed. 'It's also handy for carrying house guests and their luggage up to the house. The guests are very impressed when they're met by a private train.'

'I'll bet they are!' Lovell said. 'We could use a narrow-gauge up at Blaney Hall. I'll look into it after the war. Perhaps I'll be able to offer you a job, Lieutenant. You could help me plan it.'

Hawker beamed with pleasure.

'I'm sure you'd find it worthwhile. Of course it's quite a large capital outlay, but that won't be a problem to *you*, sir.'

Lovell peered ahead through the left-hand viewing port.

'Absolutely not!' he said.

Wren and Bass settled themselves inside the box-wagon. It was full of sacks of potatoes. They made themselves seats and as soon as the train started to move, Wren closed the sliding door. He took out his cigarettes and they lit up.

Jacko inhaled deeply and let the smoke out in a great sigh. He looked at Wren intently.

'Well, Charlie,' he said, 'what do you think of Lovell after that business with the sentry?'

'He did what had to be done,' Wren replied, 'and he did it well.'

'He enjoyed it,' Bass said flatly.

Wren shrugged.

'So he's got a twisted sense of humour. At least he doesn't believe in playing the game like the rest of the bloody officer class. War's not a game; it's a street bundle. You hit the other bloke when he's not looking, kick him when he's down and piss off quick before his mates turn up. Lovell knows that. If he can have a laugh while he's doing it, that's all right by me. I'd rather him than a hundred of the other kind.'

'You still don't understand it, do you?' Bass said, shaking his head. 'With him it's not a question of doing what has to be done. It's meat and drink to him. He's an out and out bastard and he'd just as soon do it to me or you as to some poor bloody Hun.'

But Wren didn't believe it. He was convinced that Jacko's hatred of Lovell was clouding his judgement.

Bass looked at him bitterly.

'All right, Charlie,' he said finally, 'have it your own way. But I'm telling you straight: I know him. He's up to something. I can tell the way he keeps laughing to himself.'

Wren grinned and Jacko grew angry.

'Listen! If you're smart you'll listen to what I'm saying. If funny things start happening, just remember he's up to something. And whatever you do, don't trust him, Charlie!'

11

Back to foot-slogging. A mile or so back, Hawker had spotted lights in the distance and Lovell ordered the train to be stopped. Hawker had halted the engine and allowed the others to get off, then regretfully, but at the captain's insistence, he reversed the gears and sent the train back the way it had come. Lovell wanted no clue left as to where they had got off.

'Bye, bye, Hellmuth,' Hawker called sadly, as he stepped down from the footplate and watched the driverless engine begin its headlong journey.

At some point it would smash into buffers or other traffic on the line, but Hawker's concern was for the little loco rather than the men it might crush and maim.

The steep banks of the cutting gave good cover as they followed the railway line on foot. The night was dark but star shells burned brightly overhead and there was intermittant shelling. As they approached a blind bend, Lovell halted them with a raised hand and went forward to take a look.

Minutes later, the captain reappeared again and addressed them in low tones.

'Now listen carefully,' he said. 'Just around this bend is the entrance to a brigade command post dugout. It'll be full of Huns directing the defences of Flers.'

'Point taken, sir,' Wren said. 'Give it a wide berth. Get past quickly.'

He was keen to get on.

Lovell smiled.

'No, sergeant, I'm afraid we're not giving it a wide berth.'

'We're not, sir?'

'No, we're not. In fact we're going inside.'

Lovell chuckled, then laughed outright at the looks on their faces. Hawker smiled inanely, Wren stared in disbelief and Bass took two steps backwards as if disassociating himself from the whole business.

'How come, sir?' Wren asked beligerently.

'When Sir John Trent briefed you about this job,' Lovell explained, 'he told you that Sir Douglas Haig would only allow it to go ahead on the condition that we make a direct contribution to the main attack. That contribution is to destroy this command post and thus cause a major disruption in the German defences.'

'How many Huns are in there, sir? Wren asked.

Lovell shrugged.

'I don't know. At least half a dozen. Maybe a dozen.'

'Bloody hell, sir! Wren protested. 'We can do without that. This job's hard enough as it is!'

'Christ almighty!' Bass muttered disgustedly.

'Don't worry, Jacko,' Lovell said spitefully, 'you won't be going in.'

Hawker drew his automatic.

'How do you propose we tackle it, sir?' he asked.

'Bravo Lieutenant!' Lovell laughed, then he spoke more seriously. 'Look,' he said, 'I don't like this any more than you do, but orders are orders. We've got no choice. Sergeant Wren and I will go inside and do what has to be done. Lieutenant Hawker and Private Bass will wait outside. Their job will be to deal with any Huns that might avoid our attentions and escape from the dugout.' He watched doubtfully as Jacko drew his big revolver. 'But for goodness' sake be careful,' Lovell added. 'Don't shoot each other and don't shoot the sergeant and me when we come out.'

The command post was easily identified by the thick bunches of telephone cable leading into its sandbagged entrance. As they approached a German runner emerged looking tired and nervous. He gave them a cursory glance and trotted off on his dangerous business.

'Lucky man!' Lovell muttered. He drew and checked his pistols. 'Sergeant Wren,' he said tersely, 'give me five seconds, then follow me in.'

'No, sir,' Wren said.

'What?'

Wren gripped the shotgun and levered a cartridge into the breach.

'With respect, sir, when I go in with this gun I don't want any friends in front of me. I have to go first.'

Lovell looked at the outsized muzzle of the Winchester. He nodded briefly.

'Very well. When you get inside, move to your left. I'll count five and follow you in. I'll be on your right.'

A canvas curtain hung over the dugout's doorway. Wren hooked it aside with the barrel of the shotgun and stepped inside.

Wren believed he was going alone into an armed enemy camp. He expected that, in the next instant, every German inside would be pointing a weapon in his direction. But the scene that met his eyes was totally unexpected.

In the first place, no one noticed him enter. The dugout was a brigade command and communications centre. Its entire being was centred upon the map table in the centre of the room and the big telephone switchboard against one wall. All available light was focused on these two areas so that all other parts of the dugout, including the entrance, were cloaked in gloom.

After seven days of bombardment and at the end of the first day of a great battle, everyone in the room was close to exhaustion. At the table, two grey-haired officers sat facing each other. One was fast asleep in a high-backed armchair. His companion nodded over the table, a mug of coffee at his elbow, the remains of a cigarette smouldering between his fingers. Ashtrays and half-eaten snacks lay among the curling layers of maps in the bright pool of light. The man at the switchboard spoke softly into the mouthpiece on his chest, persistently repeating the same phrase in a tired voice.

One dark alcove contained a row of cots. Three men were sound asleep and one sat in the glimmer of an oil lamp writing a letter. On a long bench near the door, three runners waited for orders. Two dozed with their chins on their chests; the other slumped lethargically over a crumpled newspaper.

Wren saw all this in two seconds. There were ten men in the dugout; all of them defenceless. In another three seconds Captain Lovell would follow him in.

Wren stopped thinking, raised the shotgun and fired. The first blast killed the telephonist and smashed his board; the second and third killed the men at the table. He continued firing, closing his mind to the shrieks and the nightmare faces as the sleeping men awoke to terror. At some point, when the Winchester's hammer had fallen twice on an empty chamber, Wren registered that the captain was beside him, a pistol blazing in both hands, a look of exultation on his face.

As Wren backed towards the doorway, groping in his pockets for fresh cartridges, the rapid fire ceased and was replaced by a dreadful silence. Lovell moved deliberately around the dugout, seeking people out, firing single shots as he mopped up.

Wren was the first to emerge, looking white-faced and shaken. Hawker started forward eagerly.

'How did it go, Charlie?'

Before Hawker's cheerful smile Wren felt an overwhelming shame at what they had done. He stepped in front of Hawker, barring his way.

'Don't go in there, sir,' Wren said desperately, and ended lamely: 'They put up quite a fight.'

Captain Lovell came out reloading his pistols. At Wren's remark he laughed roundly as if it was a good joke.

'Hawker,' he said, 'if I had ten men like Sergeant Wren, I'd raid Berlin.'

And he laughed again, shaking his head in appreciation of the moment.

Lovell and Wren took Mills bombs from their webbing, pulled the pins and tossed them carefully through the dugout door. There were muffled explosions.

'Sir!' Jacko Bass hissed and they all turned as a lone German appeared out of the gloom and advanced down the cutting towards them.

It was a young field officer on his way to to the command post. When he saw Lovell's group and the black smoke billowing from the doorway he stopped dead and put his hand on his pistol.

Lovell waved a greeting but the man still hesitated.

'*Alles klar?*' he called suspiciously.

'*Ja, ja,*' Lovell replied cheerily and went to meet him, his right hand raised in greeting, the short-barrelled Webley held casually behind his back.

As they came together, Lovell shot the man in the face at close range then shot him twice more as he fell to the ground. As he rejoined the group he was grinning and his eyes were bright.

'I think we've done our bit for Duggie Haig,' he said. 'Let's get on.'

12

'Well, gentlemen,' Captain Lovell said softly, 'at last I can tell you why we're here. In 1914 I hid a fortune in jewels in the crypt of Flers church.'

They were crouching in the mouth of an ancient tunnel looking out onto the main street of Flers village. The tunnel led from the northern outskirts close to the deep railway cutting and emerged in the southern end of the main street. It had been dug three centuries ago, when terror stalked the land. Mercenary bands could strike without warning, looting and killing. At such times, prudent communities tended to provide themselves with a hiding place and escape route.

In 1914, the occupying Germans soon found the tunnel and put it to good use. They had also improved it, installing ventilation shafts in the roof and sandbagged emergency exits at frequent intervals. Storage 'caves' had been dug in the tunnel walls and both entrances had been widened for easy access and strengthened with timber supports.

Lovell spoke again in low tones.

'Out of here we go to the left,' he said. 'The church is a couple of hundred yards further up the street.'

As they watched, an enemy infantry formation in column of twos tramped its way past the tunnel entrance and headed down the main street towards the front line positions. A salvo of shells whistled overhead and exploded somewhere in the village. The Germans edged closer to the buildings and broke into a run.

'Come on!' Lovell hissed, and seizing the moment, they sprinted from the tunnel, purposefully carrying their shovels and telephone wire.

The church was on the right side of the road directly around the next bend. It was in surprisingly good condition. The top half of the spire had been knocked down and fallen masonry littered the steps and both sides of the street, but all four walls were untouched. The front doors were intact and open. Lovell entered cautiously but the building seemed deserted. Gaping holes in the roof and fallen debris littering the nave indicated that the church was still a prime target for British guns.

The captain hurried down the left-hand aisle and paused where a flight of stone steps and a full-sized doorway led to the crypt. He waved them on impatiently and disappeared through the door. Lovell's companions were nervous as they entered, but they needn't have worried. Crypts are not really playgrounds of the living dead. They are places of utility; extensions of the church giving increased working space and storage.

The first impression was of height and space; there was no need to duck or stoop. The crypt ran the whole length of the church, the roof being supported by three rows of pillars: one lining each side wall and a single row down the centre. The pillars themselves were no taller then a man but the vaulted ceiling arched upwards until it was 12 feet at its highest point.

When Lovell first visited the church in 1914 the crypt was lit by daylight from ground-level windows. The main difference now, was in the light – or the lack of it. The Germans had piled sandbags against all windows and the darkness was total.

Lovell switched on his torch. They clustered nervously behind him, their footsteps on the stone flags echoing eerily around the pillars and vaults. Following his torch beam, the captain led them confidently to the far end of the crypt. There, laid end to end on a wide shelf cut at waist-height into the wall, were a number of ancient stone coffins. Lovell stopped beside the smallest one, a tiny coffin about three feet long.

'This is it!' he called.

The captain unslung his haversack and placed it on the floor. The torchlight flashed on the stone lid of the coffin. There was some kind of carving on it. Lovell grasped the lid and heaved sideways; it moved with a heavy scraping sound. Lovell shone his torch inside and rummaged with his free hand.

'It's still here!' he cried jubilantly and they saw him heave a pair of heavy saddlebags out of the coffin and rest them on the corner of the open end.

As they crowded round, he unbuckled the flaps of the saddlebags and began to lift handful after handful of precious stones into the light.

The torch shone like a searchlight on the cascade of gems: diamonds as bright as star shells, gas-green emeralds, rubies like drops of blood. There were necklaces and brace-lets; rings and clasps; the flash of silver and the gleam of gold. Lovell grinned at them proudly, like a conjuror pluck-ing silk handkerchiefs from the air and casting them into his hat. For a full minute, the jewels held them breathless at the beauty and fortune before them. Then a salvo of heavy shells bumped to earth nearby, making the walls tremble and trickles of dust to fall from the roof. The spell was broken.

Lovell rebuckled the saddlebags and made to close the coffin lid but the torch slipped from his grasp and fell to the floor. The beam stayed on and they saw it rolling across the flagstones.

'I'll get it, sir!' Hawker cried, and scrambled forward.

He recovered the torch and handed it to the captain.

'Thanks,' Lovell said. 'It's time we got out of here. Hawker, you carry the swag.'

He swung the saddlebags to Hawker, who was caught by surprise and almost dropped them.

'Heavy!' Hawker said.

'Yes, that's the gold,' Lovell replied. 'I had to bend the tiaras flat I'm afraid, but a good goldsmith will soon have them as good as new.'

Hawker hoisted the saddlebags onto one shoulder and Lovell dragged the coffin lid back into place.

'Nanny always said: "Leave things as you found them"!' he said cheerfully.

'Is it a child's coffin, sir?' Wren asked thickly.

The thought had been with him for some time and he had to ask.

'No,' Lovell replied. 'Though you'd think so if you didn't know any better. In the old days when a rich traveller died abroad, it wasn't practical to bring the body home. So they removed certain significant parts – the heart, the hands, that sort of thing – preserved them in brandy or brine and brought them home. Then the bits were buried or interred in one of these little coffins. But I chose it because I thought the Huns would probably take it for a child's coffin and leave it alone.' He shone his torch again on the closed lid. 'Also,' he said, 'it's got this carving on it. I think it's supposed to be a lion but it looks more like a dog.' Lovell grinned. 'I thought it very appropriate.'

The captain picked up his haversack.

'Right, we've got what we came for, let's get moving.'

He shone his light on the the flagstones and led the way

out. They followed him in single file to the doorway and steps, and up into the main body of the church.

On the darkened battlefield Bob Tyke woke stiff and cold. His head ached and his mouth was like sandpaper. He drank deeply from his water bottle and peered at his wristwatch with one good eye. It was eleven thirty. He had five hours to make his way back to the British lines. *Plenty of time*, he thought, but as he gathered himself for the task he shivered and his limbs felt like jelly.

He raised his head cautiously, seeking the lie of the land. He must get his direction right. It would be a real bastard if he crawled into the Hun lines by mistake and the thought made him snort briefly in amusement.

From behind both front lines, searchlights played on low cloud, bathing the battlefield in unreal light. Star shells rose and fell in the sky, casting creeping shadows, causing the grotesque shapes of no man's land to shift and waver. Machine-guns stuttered lazily in short bursts and there was a background rumble of distant guns.

Tyke got ready. He would have to crawl all the way – 200 yards at least. Probably a lot further avoiding exposed patches and circumventing shell craters. He discarded everything but his water bottle, even putting his helmet aside. After some experimentation, he hung his water bottle crossways from one shoulder and tightened it beneath his armpit so that it wouldn't swing and impede his progress. Pleased with his preparation, Tyke waited for the star shells to wane then started forward.

He had gone ten yards when, without warning, a star shell burst directly overhead turning night into day. Tyke froze like a lizard in mid-crawl, but a sniper's bullet cracked past his ear and a machine-gun began to hammer, kicking up a fountain of earth that advanced towards him. Tyke rolled clumsily sideways. He knew he had no chance and braced himself for the agony of bullets ripping into his flesh. But in the next second the ground fell steeply away and he threw himself downwards. He grinned with relief as bullets cracked overhead, but in the next second the breath was knocked from his body as he plunged into a an icy pool of stagnant water. He went in head first and came up retching. He had blundered into a shell hole. The pool was thick with liquid chalk and putrid with chemical scum and human body parts. Shuddering in fear and disgust, Tyke stood waist-deep and floundered to the edge. Desperation propelled him up the churned sides of the crater and at last he crawled thankfully into a deep fissure at the top.

Tyke was beaten before he had started. In five minutes his feeling of confidence and resolve had changed to one of depression and self-pity. He had been sure he could reach the British lines under cover of night. But there *was* no cover. Seachlights and star shells turned night into day. The only darkness was in stinking pits filled with slime and decomposing bodies. He trembled uncontrollably with shock and cold. His head ached and pain from the eye that was no longer there stabbed like a needle into his brain. He crept closer to the earth, rolled himself into a ball and hugged the wet clothes to his shivering body. In doing so he felt the hardness of the water bottle under his arm. It was still half-full. He rinsed his mouth with water and rubbed some over his face, shuddering at the memory of the putrid pool closing over his head.

He lay there shivering, half-heartedly debating with himself what to do. At the moment he was in no state to do anything except keep his head down. Crawling to his own lines just wasn't practical. On the other hand, a new day might bring further developments and some unexpected relief. Stay put, that was his best bet. Tyke nodded to himself in agreement. He would wait for the morning.

13

They were back in the tunnel.

Once out of the crypt, Lovell had taken the saddlebags from Hawker and stowed them in his pack. The short journey back from the church had been uneventful. Shelling of the village had increased as the main British barrage crept closer. The Germans in the village were keeping their heads down and steeling themselves for the coming battle.

Earlier, on their way to the church, Captain Lovell's attention had been drawn to the many storage 'caves' dug into the tunnel walls. He considered them an ideal place to lie up and wait for the British attack to reach Flers. They had therefore returned to the tunnel.

Lovell and Wren made a careful exploration. Many of the caves lay down subsidiary tunnels with chamber after chamber cut deep into the chalk. All of them were packed with provisions, munitions and supplies. After a close inpection, Lovell selected one whose contents seemed the least likely to be required. He collected Hawker and Bass and led them in by the light of his torch.

'We'd have to be be very unlucky for the Huns to visit this one in the next couple of days.' Lovell pronounced drolly, surveying huge quantities of harness, saddle-soap, and horse gas masks. 'What d'you think, Hawker?'

'Looks perfect, sir,' Hawker laughed. 'We'll take it!'

'Good, let's have some grub,' Lovell said. 'Move yourself, Jacko!'

Bass lit his lamp and hauled out the rations. There were Bath Oliver biscuits, pressed brisket of beef, and sausages in tomato sauce. They were all ravenous after the long day's exertions and attacked the food like hungry wolves. Finally they had eaten their fill, washed it down with water and made to turn in for the night.

'Any whisky left, Jacko,' Lovell asked.

'A drop, sir,'

'Good, we need a good night's rest.'

Bass gave them all a good measure and made to include himself.

'Not you, Jacko,' Lovell said, taking the bottle away and setting it on the floor. 'You take first guard duty. I'll relieve you at two o'clock. You can have your tot then.'

Hawker and Wren used their packs as pillows and rolled themseves in their blankets.

Lovell picked up his haversack and swung it across to Hawker.

'I'm taking second watch,' he said. 'You chaps had better look after the loot. Guard it well.'

'Right, sir,' Hawker said.

He placed the haversack on the floor between himself and Wren. As an afterthought, he unfastened one of the straps and threaded it through the straps of his own and Wren's pack, effectively tying all three packs together.

Lovell gently mocked Hawker's caution.

'Belt and Braces, Lieutenant,' he chuckled, 'Belt and Braces.'

He led Jacko Bass out of the cave and showed him the sentry point close to the main tunnel.

A few minutes later, already half-asleep, Hawker and Wren heard the captain return, extinguish the lamp and settle down to rest.

The next thing Wren knew, the lamp was lit and Lovell was shaking him awake. Beside him, Hawker was sitting up in his blankets rubbing the sleep from his eyes.

'Wake up, Sergeant,' Lovell hissed urgently. 'Private Bass is missing. I can't find him anywhere!'

'He can't be far away, sir,' Wren replied irritably. 'Perhaps he's answering a call of nature.'

The captain shook his head.

'I thought perhaps he went into one of the other caves for that reason but there's no sign of him anywhere.'

Lovell stopped at a sudden thought.

'The jewels!' he said frantically. 'Check the haversack!'

But Hawker was ahead of him. He had already opened the haversack and laid his hand on the leather saddlebags inside.

'It's all right, sir,' he said easily. 'They're here.'

'Thank heaven for that!' Lovell said fervently. He made to walk away, then turned back. 'You'd better check properly,' he told Hawker.

Hawker grinned, unbuckled the saddle bags and peered inside.

'What is it? What's wrong?' Lovell cried.

Hawker had stopped grinning. His mouth fell open and he gaped from Lovell to Wren with an expression of confusion and disbelief.

Lovell wrenched the saddlebags from his grasp and rummaged inside. Then, with a gesture of despair, he turned them upside down, spilling their contents onto the floor.

The jewels were gone. In their place was a choice selection of iron rations: tinned ox-tongue; pressed brisket of beef; sausages in tomato sauce; Fry's Five Boys chocolate – all the items Jacko had carried in his pack.

Lovell exploded in rage.

'That filthy, thieving little swine,' he snarled. 'I'll kill him! I'll chop him into little pieces!'

110

He kicked at the empty saddlebags and rushed from the cave in vain pursuit of the criminal.

In a daze, Hawker examined the haversack which had contained the jewels and found that it was still strapped to the other two packs. He picked up one of the fallen items and scrutinised a tin of sausages as if he had never seen its like before.

The irony of it all slapped Wren in the face. He threw back his head and laughed. Jacko the clown, Jacko the pack mule, Jacko the waste of space had fooled them all. He had taken the one chance he had and got away with a fortune in jewels, leaving in their place the mountain of provisions Lovell had forced him to carry for so many miles. Wren's wild laughter echoed through the cave in salute to the little man whose unlikely defiance had turned a brilliant operation into a comic farce.

14

'Can you see *any* of our chaps, sir,' Hawker asked anxiously.

'Not a single one,' Captain Lovell replied, peering through his binoculars.

Lovell, Hawker and Wren crouched in a German support trench on a ridge close to Serre and looked across no man's land towards the British lines.

After Jacko Bass and the jewels had disappeared, Lovell wasn't prepared to hang around waiting for the British army to reach Flers. He was concerned that Bass might somehow cross the lines and get away to the coast with the jewels.

The captain wanted to get back to the army as quickly as possible and raise the alarm. He decided that the quickest way to achieve this was to retrace their route to Serre which was scheduled for capture on the first day of the 'Big Push'. With the German line breached and in the confusion of a breakthrough, it should be a relatively simple matter to meet up with the army again.

It had been hard going. Without the use of a train they had to footslog the whole way and the return journey took longer. But Lovell drove them mercilessly in his determination to regain British territory ahead of Jacko Bass, and alert the authorities to the theft of the jewels.

No one challenged the small party striding earnestly along carrying their shovels and coil of telephone wire.

Work parties were everywhere: clearing debris; rebuilding roads; repairing trenches and dugouts. They had ditched their packs and carried only weapons, water and chocolate. They did the whole journey in six hours. It was 8.00 a.m.

Lovell passed the glasses to Hawker, who swept them carefully over the ground. Just forward of the British front line he could see neat rows of British army packs lying in the long grass. Triangular scraps of tin tied to the packs sparkled in the sun.

'It looks as if the Pals left most of their packs in no man's land,' Hawker said. 'So as to get across quicker, I suppose.'

He handed the binoculars to Charlie Wren.

Wren took the glasses and followed Hawker's pointing finger. Perhaps Bob Tyke had taken his advice and the first wave had left their packs behind. After a moment Wren lowered the binoculars thoughtfully, then reluctantly looked again, not wanting to confirm what he had seen.

'I'm afraid that's not the case, sir,' he said at last. 'They're packs all right, but the Pals are still wearing them. It looks as if they were wiped out almost before they started.'

'You're right, sergeant,' Captain Lovell agreed. 'And that's why we didn't meet any British troops on the way here. I'm afraid the attack here was a complete failure. The whole of this ridge is still held by the Huns.'

'How are we going to get back then, sir?' Wren asked.

'I don't know,' Lovell replied. 'Let's get closer.'

Still wearing their coal-scuttle helmets and carrying their tools they were able to move right into the forward trenches. From there they could clearly see that the Pals had lost the battle. Hundreds of dead and wounded lay in no man's land. With painful slowness they were being tended and collected by stretcher-bearers who systematically worked their way across the battlefield. A truce was in place and the Germans were allowing the British to move around unhin-

113

dered. The British defeat had been so crushing; and the scene inspired such pity, that German stretcher-bearers could also be seen working, wearing their big helmets and white Red Cross armbands.

'Perhaps we could wait here all day, sir,' Wren suggested, 'Get across at night.'

Lovell shook his head.

'No. There seems to be a truce in force at the moment, but I can't see it lasting all day. And anyway, once it gets dark the Huns will be on their mettle again. They'll fire at the slightest movement.'

But Hawker already had the anwer. Chuckling with excitement, he took his Number One Field Dressing from his breast pocket and tied it around Wren's left arm above the elbow.

Lovell grinned and shook his head in admiration.

'Hawker,' he said, 'you bird-men never cease to amaze me!'

A few moments later, Lovell took a deep breath, climbed out of the trench and stood upright on the parapet.

'Right,' he said. 'Follow me.'

Hawker and Wren climbed up beside him and together they walked casually into no man's land.

Bob Tyke had been awake for hours. He was weaker than ever and his water was finished. In the first hour of daylight, a renewed bombardment of the Britiish front line showed that the Germans feared a continuation of the attack. But firing soon ceased altogether. Tyke knew he couldn't last much longer. There had been no firing or shelling for over an hour and he decided to take a chance.

With the last of his strength, he hauled himself out of the damp fissure he had been lying in and crawled into the sunlight. Looking towards the British lines, he could see stretcher-bearers working freely in the open. There must be some kind of truce.

Propping himself into a sitting position, he looked around him. The Germans were helping the wounded too. He could see them moving about in their big helmets and white armbands. He was about half-way across no man's land and hoped the British would reach him before the Huns.

But his luck was out again. The Germans got to him first – three of them with grubby, unshaven, surprisingly friendly faces. His surprise increased as they lifted him onto a stretcher improvised from leather jerkins and two long-handled shovels. As far as he could tell they seemed to be taking him to the British lines, but he couldn't be sure because by then he was delirious. He knew he must be delirious because one of the Hun stretcher-bearers was wearing Royal Flying Corps shoulder tags and looked exactly like Charlie Wren.

PART 2

15

'And when he'd finished, he said to the girl: "Darling, am I you're first lover?" "Well," she said, "you could be. You look familiar!"'

Charlie Wren chuckled briefly and moved away from the crowd around the sailor telling jokes at the bar. Carefully guarding his pint, he pushed his way through the press of bodies to the side passage and towards the saloon. He had arranged to meet his sister Lizzie and her husband Fred here in the Fish and Ring on Mile End Road.

After they had returned to the British lines posing as German stretcher-bearers, Lovell, Hawker and Wren had travelled to Amiens for a debriefing with Sir John Trent. Thereafter, they had all been sent on a week's leave.

Lovell had reported the failure of their mission and named Jacko Bass as the culprit. Bass was posted as a fugitive wanted for desertion and theft. Wren had said nothing at the debriefing but the whole business puzzled him. Jacko had been terrified of Lovell. Wren couldn't believe he'd found the nerve to desert behind enemy lines and take the jewels with him.

Then there was the business of the Jacko's Shakespear Knife. When they had first discovered the jewels were missing and Lovell had rushed out into the tunnel, Wren had kicked dejectedly at Jacko's bed-roll that lay ready on the floor. As he moved the rolled poncho Jacko used as a pillow, the sheathed Shakespear Knife had fallen out. Wren had quickly scooped it up and stowed it inside his tunic. Now he found it strange that Bass hadn't taken the knife with him. Jacko kept the weapon with him always. It was like a talisman to him – his last ditch defence. And yet he had left it behind.

Later, on their way to catch the leave boat at Boulogne, Wren had raised the subject quietly with Hawker.

Hawker's reaction was to stare wide-eyed in astonishment.

'You amaze me, Charlie,' he said. 'Are you saying there's some doubt in your mind that Private Bass absconded with the jewels?'

'Yes, sir,' Wren said stoically.

'But, Charlie,' Hawker explained patiently, 'there were only four of us there. If you don't believe Private Bass is guilty and if you rule out ourselves . . .' He hesitated, 'You *do* rule out present company I hope.'

Wren smiled.

'Yes, sir.'

'Then the only remaining suspect is Captain Lovell himself,' Hawker concluded.

'Yes, sir,' Wren said.

Hawker laughed wildly.

'You can't mean that!' he said incredulously.

'It's not impossible, sir,' said Wren.

'My dear Watson,' Hawker said, shaking his head pityingly, 'even Inspector Lestrade on an off day will tell you that any criminal suspect must be deemed to have had opportunity and motive. Even taking the first as read – because he was there – where is Captain Lovell's motive? He's the direct heir to the Blaney title and fortune. He's got no need for a few pieces of jewelry.'

'It was a bit more than that, sir,' Wren said drily.

'Even so,' Hawker went on, 'who's the most likely suspect, Captain Lovell or a penniless private? And don't forget Bass is a convicted thief. The military police checked his background and turned up a record as long as your arm.'

'I know, sir,' Wren sighed.

'There you are, then,' Hawker said dismissively. 'Best forget about it, Charlie. You'll only cause trouble for yourself making wild accusations. Private Bass has either fallen into the hands of the hated Hun or he'll be caught and tried by our own people. Either way, it's out of our hands now.'

'Yes, sir,' Wren said dutifully and let the matter drop.

But privately it continued to trouble him. He had to admit that the bare facts supported Hawker's view. It was possible that Jacko had finally cracked under Lovell's abuse of him or that the sight of a fortune in jewels had been too big a temptation. But Wren *knew* Jacko. To imagine him creeping into the cave where they were all sleeping, taking the jewels and replacing them with tinned food was laughable. And yet there seemed to be no alternative explanation.

Wren had racked his memory over the sequence of events. The jewels were in the saddlebags; everyone had seen Lovell take them out of the stone coffin. Hawker had carried them out of the crypt; and they had all watched Lovell stow the saddlebags in his pack. From that moment the pack was never out of their sight. And when Jacko disappeared, so did the jewels. It was a mystery and Wren hoped a week's leave would help him forget about it.

When he finally shouldered his way through the saloon door, he looked around in surprise. The room was full of women. Groups of ten or a dozen women and young girls packed the tables, drinking and smoking, talking loudly and shrieking with hysterical laughter.

As he stood in the doorway, laughing faces turned towards him and there were coarse cries of, ''E's a bit of alright!', 'Over 'ere, Luvvie!' and 'I saw 'im first!'

121

Wren was about to retreat when a man's voice cut in urgently, 'Charlie, Charlie! Over here!'

Lizzie and Fred and another man were seated at a corner table.

'We've saved you a seat,' Lizzie said, as Fred slid in with her on the bench seat, leaving an empty chair for Wren.

'This is Roy,' Lizzie said, indicating the stranger. 'Roy, this is Charlie, my lickle bruvver.'

'Pleased to meet you, Charlie,' Roy said.

He was a dapper character dressed in a checked suit and bow tie. He looked out of place with Fred and Lizzie.

Fred was a shy, insignificant little man who only seemed to come alive when he'd had a drink. Years before, he had broken his leg in a factory accident and had limped badly ever since. He scraped a living selling matches and bootlaces from a pitch in the City and took horse racing bets on the side. He was a good father to the two children and Lizzie thought the world of him. Wren liked his brother-in-law well enough but he'd always thought that his sister could have done better for herself. Lizzie had been a beauty as a young girl and was bright and intelligent, but life with Fred and the children had jaded her. She could still look good when she took the trouble and Wren was very fond of her and enjoyed her company.

Wren had difficulty making himself heard above the noise. He looked around irritably.

'This place is too crowded,' he complained. 'Can't we go somewhere else? What about the Raglan?'

'The Raglan'll be no different,' Lizzie said. 'The factory girls are out in force. Now we've got seats we might as well stay put.'

'That's Flying Corps, isn't it, Charlie?' Roy asked politely, indicating Wren's observer's brevet.

'That's right,' Wren replied.

122

'Shot down any Zeppelins yet, Charlie?' Fred said with a laugh.

'Nah,' Wren replied. 'Don't see them in France.'

'We see plenty over here!' Fred said excitedly. 'People have been killed by them.'

'Not a lot, though,' Wren said. 'They'll never be a real threat. They're too prone to the weather.'

'They were a threat to Danny Smith,' Lizzie put in hotly. 'They blew his head off!'

'Who?' Wren said.

'Danny Smith, a bloke who works at our place,' Lizzie replied. 'The Zeppelins were bombing and Danny was standing in the doorway of the Lamb and Lion holding a pint. A bomb came and blew his head off!'

'It didn't blow his head *off*, love,' Fred said gently. 'His head was bashed in by a bloody great piece of iron.'

'He was still dead,' Lizzie said pointedly

'I know he was, love, ' Fred said. 'But I don't think it was a bomb that did it. Our guns were going and it was more likely a bit of one of our own shells. When those guns blaze away they do more damage than the old Zeps. I'm right, aren't I Charlie?'

'I expect so,' Wren said.

'Stands to reason,' Fred went on. 'The shrapnel from the shells comes down like hailstones. You can hear it hitting the roof tiles. You can see it in the streets the morning after: shrapnel balls, pieces of shell cases, what goes up must come down. I'm right, aren't I Charlie?'

'I expect so,' Wren said.

'Stands to reason,' Fred nodded emphatically.

'And Danny is still dead,' Lizzie said drily.

'War's a terrible thing,' Fred said profoundly. Then brightly and in the same breath, he added, 'What's it like in France, Charlie?'

Wren laughed ironically and Lizzie looked at him and laid a hand on his arm.

'Is it really terrible out there, Charlie?' she asked anxiously.

Wren looked at her with affection.

'Nah,' he grinned. 'France is all right – if it doesn't kill you!'

Fred looked at them uncomfortably and got to his feet.

'Excuse me while I go and shake hands with the vicar,' he said formally.

'Get some more drinks while you're at it,' Wren said, handing him half a crown.

'Right,' Fred said. 'Back in a trice!'

'I'll come with you, Mrs Shoe,' Roy said, and followed him out, both of them laughing at some private joke.

Wren looked at Lizzie.

'How's my old skin and blister? he asked gently.

'All right, Charlie,' she said smiling.

'Happy?'

'Yes, Charlie, we're fine. With my job at the factory, we're better off now than we've ever been. Fred does well, too. With the war, there's a lot more money about. How about you?'

'I'm all right,' Wren said shortly.

He drained his glass and lit a cigarette.

Lizzie watched him silently for a moment, then she said, 'I saw Fran the other day.'

'Fran?' Wren said distantly as if trying to put a face to the name.

'Fran, your wife,' Lizzie said drily. 'Fran, the woman you're married to. She works at the factory. I saw her in the tram queue.'

'How is she, then,' Wren said finally.

'She's surviving – just. She'll never be the same, Charlie,

and you can't expect her to be. A woman never gets over a thing like that.'

'It's been known to knock some men about a bit too!' Wren said hotly.

'Not the same as a woman, Charlie,' Lizzie asserted. 'With a woman, it's part of her gone forever.'

'Where have those two got to?' Wren said desperately, craning for sight of the returning Roy and Fred. He got to his feet hurriedly. 'I'm going to get some more drinks.'

'All right,' Lizzie said indignantly, 'but when you come back, Fran will still be your wife!'

Wren met the other two in the corridor, still laughing and triumphantly carrying a tray of drinks each.

'It's murder in there,' Fred explained cheerfully. 'We got three rounds to save time.'

The three sat down, Wren glaring his sister into silence.

'Before you got here, Charlie,' Fred said, 'we were telling Roy about the show we saw last night. It was pretty good.'

'It was wonderful,' Lizzie said, cheering up. 'A real variety show. There was a bit of everything.'

'I liked the magic act,' Fred said. 'That conjurer bloke was good. You'd have appreciated him, Roy.' Fred turned to Charlie. 'Roy does magic,' he explained.

'He wasn't a conjurer, Fred,' Lizzie insisted. 'He was an illusionist. The Great Mugglèstoné he was called. You know,' Lizzie explained, 'spelt like French with little things over the "E"s.' She wrote in the air with her forefinger. 'The Great Mugglèstoné, Emperor of Illusion.' Lizzie said grandly. 'He was amazing!'

'Oh I know Mugglestonnay,' Roy laughed, drawing the name out. 'But he's not French. He was born round the corner in Shandy Street, two doors away from us. His name's Tommy Mugglestone. You must know him, Fred.

His dad, Fuzzy Mugglestone, used to play a barrel organ outside Mile End station.'

'I remember Fuzzy,' Fred said slowly. 'That was Mugglè-stoné's dad?'

'The very same,' Roy laughed. 'When we were kids, me and Tommy used to practise our magic together. Sorry to spoil it for you, Lizzie,' he added.

Lizzie looked as if her world had come to an end.

'He was still good,' she said defiantly.

'He was,' Fred agreed. 'That big stunt at the end with the girl and the pigeons was marvellous.'

'Doves,' Lizzie corrected.

'What?' said Fred.

'Doves! They weren't pigeons, they were doves. Doves of peace.'

'They were?' Fred said vaguely.

Lizzie sighed in exasperation.

'You didn't get the point at all, did you?' She explained it to her husband patiently, using both hands. 'The girl was dressed as Britannia. She was meant to be Britain. She went into the cabinet which was done up in the French colours: red, white and blue. The cabinet was meant to be France. As the cabinet rose in the air, there were all those bangs and flashes. That was the war. Are you still with me, Fred?'

Fred nodded vaguely. Wren and Roy laughed.

'Then the curtain with "Victory" written on it came down over the cabinet. The curtain fell, and all the doves of peace flew out of the cabinet and the girl had disappeared. There was silence for a bit and then the girl walked onto the stage with the band playing 'Rule Brittania.' Lizzie spread her hands and smiled as if she had just performed it herself.

'Hooray!' Roy cried and clapped ironically.

'Sounds like the old "girl in the box" trick to me,' Wren said.

'It *was* good though,' Fred asserted. 'I mean, you could

see the girl in the cabinet. And then, in a second, she'd gone and the pigeons – sorry doves,' he glanced sheepishly at his wife, 'and the doves were there instead. And the cabinet was suspended in the air. I mean how could the girl have got out? It beats me,' he said finally.

'It was magic,' Roy said with a smile.

'It seemed like it at the time,' Lizzie laughed.

'And that's what matters,' Roy said. 'You had a magical evening and came away happy and amazed. That's what it's all about.' He nodded seriously. 'Tommy's good. He's done well for himself. Good luck to him.'

'But you can't help wondering how he does it,' Fred said.

'Of course you can't,' Roy replied. 'That's all part of it.'

'Do *you* know how he did it,' Fred insisted.

'I suppose I'd know if I saw it,' Roy said.

'How, then?' Fred demanded. 'Lizzie told you what happened. Tell us how he did it.'

Roy laughed.

'I'm not going to spoil it for you. And I can't give anything away. I'm sworn to secrecy – by the brotherhood.' He tapped his nose with a forefinger. 'But I'll show you something to help you think,' he added, taking a pack of cards from the pocket of his jacket.

Fred's face lit up and he grinned at his wife.

'Oh-oh, here it comes! Watch this, Charlie!' he said eagerly.

'This is an ordinary pack of cards,' Roy said, moving easily into his magician's patter. 'I always carry it in case I meet a young lady and she fancies a quick game of strip-whist – beg pardon, Lizzie.' He unboxed the cards and shuffled them absently, the cards flowing and merging in his long fingers. 'The whole of life is an illusion,' Roy went on, addressing the three of them like some ancient sage, 'and people conspire with each other to preserve it. Some people see through the veil and glimpse the reality. But what they see is so terrible that they return quickly to illusion, and pretend they never saw the truth.'

Lizzie groaned.

'Spare us the sermon, Roy,' she said desperately.

'You want to lay off the gin, Roy,' Fred laughed. 'It's getting you down!'

'Gin's lowering,' Lizzie said knowingly.

Roy showed them the pack, holding it up like a picture in the fingers of his left hand with the bottom card towards them.

'Watch the card, closely,' he said.

It was the five of hearts. The magician began to massage the card with the index finger of his right hand. The finger moved in a circular motion with the circle growing bigger and bigger until the card was completely obscured by the palm of the right hand. Then, with a flourish the hand was drawn away and the five of hearts disappeared to be replaced by the queen of clubs. Roy repeated the movement half a dozen times and each time the facing card changed.

He ended by saying, 'Nothing up my sleeve and the hand is completely empty.'

Wren watched in admiration. Usually, he had no time for conjurers. On the stage they were too far away for you to see what was going on. But when a man did magic sitting next to you, you had to hand it to him.

'Remind me not to play cards with you, Roy.' he said, grinning.

The magician shrugged depreciatingly.

'Now watch again,' he said. 'I'll do it slowly and show you how it's done. I don't mind showing you this, because all it takes is practise. If you want to go away and practise for six months, that's all right by me.'

He took up position again, showed them the bottom card and repeated the hand movements in slow motion. Looking closely, they could just see the right hand skimming off the top card to reveal the card underneath. Roy then candidly showed them the inside of his right hand where the card had been neatly palmed.

As he said, 'Nothing up my sleeve,' his right hand brushed his left sleeve and completed a circular motion towards the top pocket of his jacket.

The palmed card dropped smoothly into the pocket and he showed them his empty right hand. 'The hand is completely empty,' he intoned.

'It's not just the quickness of the hand,' Roy explained. 'What happens is this.' And he repeated the trick again, talking them through it. 'You watch the card. I'm telling you to watch it. Then, just when the card changes, you want to look at my right hand to see if the top card is there, but see what my right hand's doing? As it palms the card, it's pointing with the index finger, and that pointing finger *holds* you, keeps you looking at the pack. You can't take your eyes away from that pointing finger!' he told them intensely. 'Ever since you were lying in your cradle, people have been pointing things out to you, "Look at the pretty flowers. Look at the puffer train. Look at that nice bit of skirt over there" – beg pardon, Lizzie – and you have to look, you can't help it. The pointing finger is the distraction – a misdirection we call it. By the time you've dragged your eyes away, the right hand is innocent again, it's clean. At the end, when I say, "Nothing up my sleeve," my voice and the sleeve is the misdirection. By the time you look at the hand again, it's clean.'

Roy showed them the empty palm, gave the cards a final shuffle and placed them on the table.

'These distractions,' Lizzie said, 'what did you call them?'

'Misdirections,' Roy said.

'These misdirections,' Lizzie went on. 'Are they used in all magic? For illusions too?'

'Of course, ' Roy replied.

'Even for the girl and the doves we saw last night?'

'Especially for those,' Roy said. 'Because in something like that, you haven't even got the quickness of the hand. Misdirections make the audience look in the wrong place, or in the right place at the wrong time. They might be simple, like I showed you – the pointing finger – or clever and complicated, depending on the nature of the illusion.'

'But there were two thousand people in that theatre,' Lizzie objected. 'How can you fool two thousand people?'

'No disrespect, Lizzie,' Roy replied easily, 'but to measure the intelligence of a crowd, you don't multiply by the number of people – you divide! Don't forget you're sitting in a darkened theatre watching a lighted stage. You were on a night out, looking for a bit of magic. It's not hard to fool people when they want to be fooled.'

Fred shook his head unhappily.

'I don't see how that can explain how the girl disappeared,' he objected.

'I'm not going to give it away,' Roy said emphatically. 'But you have to remember that when something disappears, it has to go somewhere else. If you decide it was impossible for it to go somewhere else, then perhaps it wasn't where you thought it was in the first place.'

The magician boxed his cards and put them in his pocket. He looked around at the three faces: Lizzie was clearly thinking about the girl and the doves and Fred moodily picked up his beer. Charlie Wren was staring at him intently, but his gaze seemed to go straight through him as if his mind was elsewhere. Roy watched him uneasily and forced a laugh.

'Charlie, I should know better by now. When you show somebody how magic's done, you never know how they'll react.'

'You don't?'

Charlie Wren came back to life and took a pull of his beer.

'Too right you don't,' Roy said emphatically. 'One day I showed a chap something and then, because he kept on at me, I showed him how it was done. He looked at me sulkily for a while, then he said offensive-like, "So it's just a trick, then?"' Roy shook his head in disbelief. 'I mean, what do people want, Charlie? The last miracle worker was Jesus Christ and his secrets died with him.'

The noise from the neighbouring table increased violently as the women laughed madly at some remark. The magician winced and raised his own voice in an effort to be heard.

'Why do people ask how it's done if they're going to be disappointed?' he said, looking appealingly at the three of them. 'I couldn't believe what this bloke was saying. I looked at him and I said . . .'

But the noise in the room erupted in ear-splitting crescendo as the laughter spread to other tables and the women mouthed and shrieked hysterically at each other.

Roy glanced at the ceiling in supplication and shouted desperately at Charlie Wren.

'I said to him: "Of course it was a trick! What do you expect, *bloody miracles?*"'

16

After two years of war, it could be said that the British people were divided into two distinct groups: those largely unaffected by the war whose enthusiasm for it was undiminished and who retained complete faith in the nation's ability to prevail; and another group – among them grieving parents and widows – who were becoming ever more confused and mindful of a great tragedy overshadowing their lives.

Philip Hawker's father belonged firmly to the former group. Furthermore, he seemed to have no notion of the risks his only son took daily, in pursuit of the nation's goal.

And when his wife voiced fears for her son, Mr Hawker would say impatiently, 'Philip's in the Flying Corps, dear, not in the trenches. He's up above it all.'

Not that Hawker sought to enlighten his parents as to the realities of war. Like the majority of soldiers home on leave, his instinct was to protect his loved ones from anxiety on his behalf; and his stories of army life were pale parodies of actual events; deliberately shallow and upbeat, with no bad endings.

Hawker senior's personality could best be described as 'jolly', and physically he was just a matured version of his son. The two were happily and completely compatible. So Hawker had been delighted when, on the first day of his leave, his father suggested they meet for dinner at the Royal Automobile Club in Pall Mall.

Mr Hawker's other dinner guest was Sir Rufus Strong, head of the Special Projects Department of the War Office. Sir Rufus was a huge genial man with boundless energy. He was an old friend of the Hawkers and having no son of his own – he and his wife had been blessed with five daughters – had followed the young Hawker's career with much interest and amusement.

They sat at their table in the panelled dining room of the club, surrounded by painted tributes to the automobile and portraits of action heroes past and present. Light from the chandeliers reflected gaily on the buttons and braid of the young officers crowding the tables. Sir Rufus was on especially good form, laughing uproariously at young Hawker's inane jokes and giving the general impression of being on the verge of bursting with glee.

As a concession to wartime austerity, they confined themselves to the *Table d'hôte*: celery soup; lemon sole; lamb cutlets with summer vegetables; and sherry trifle. In honour of Hawker's leave they allowed themselves the cheese board and a half-bottle of port. At last the brandy was brought and Sir Rufus and the elder Hawker availed themselves of cigars. Sir Rufus settled himself contentedly in his chair and watched young Hawker shrewdly through the smoke.

'You're a clever chap, young Philip,' he said at last. 'You've always had a bent for mechanical things. I remember you're father telling me about that motorcycle you built.'

Hawker laughed delightedly.

'Yes, sir, the old Hawker Hurricane. I wanted to put her into production and make a fortune but father wouldn't put up the money. I even offered him a half share in the profits but it was no go.' He grinned sideways at his father who smiled at the memory.

'I won't say it wasn't a good machine,' Hawker senior explained to his friend, 'but there was too much competition. In those days, every bicycle builder in the country was producing his own patent motorised machine. It wasn't just a case of production. We would have needed a network of retail outlets, an after-sales service and a major advertising campaign. You couldn't run it on mail order.'

'Just so.' Sir Rufus nodded impatiently. 'But Philip knows machines. That's my point. As a soldier, he's also aware that today's battlefield is dominated by machine-guns and barbed wire. Artillery too, of course, but the main tactical weapon of defence is the Maxim heavy machine-gun. One well-sited weapon can destroy a company; ten can stop a division; a hundred can hold up an army.'

Hawker nodded emphatically.

'Absolutely, sir. That's why we have trench warfare. Stalemate. After a preliminary artillery barrage, advances *can* be made on a narrow front, but once the attacking force outstrips its guns, attacks are broken down by the second or third lines of machine-guns and wire.'

Sir Rufus nodded.

'Exactly. What is needed is some means of flattening the enemy's wire, crossing his trenches and destroying his fortified machine-gun emplacements. Infantry can't do it. A man in an armoured suit couldn't handle the appalling terrain of no man's land. Cavalry can't do it for the same reason. Too much armour would be required for horse and rider.' Sir Rufus smiled impishly. 'Surely what's needed is some kind of machine. An armoured vehicle able to cross uneven ground, traverse trenches and barbed wire entanglements and carry soldiers equipped to deal with machine-guns in concrete emplacements.'

Sir Rufus paused to relight his cigar. When he'd got it going, he pointed it dramatically at Hawker.

'You're the engineer, Philip. How would you set about designing such a machine?'

Hawker's brow furrowed in concentration.

'Well, sir,' he said carefully. 'An ordinary wheeled vehicle would be no good. I once got bogged down in a Crossley tender and that was on the road! It would have to be some kind of track-layer. Remember the small caterpillars Captain Scott took to the Antarctic? We've got a few Holts tractors in France: 75 horsepower, petrol-driven, American made. They move the big howitzers around.'

Sir Rufus nodded, smiling cryptically.

'Go on,' he said.

'So I'd use a Holts tracked chassis,' Hawker continued, 'and above it I'd mount a big steel box to carry the soldiers. The steel box would be armour-plated and have loopholes for Lewis guns and periscopes for the driver and gunners.'

'Surely this box – this steel tank – would be vulnerable to enemy artillery,' Sir Rufus suggested.

Hawker nodded.

'It would, sir. But you asked for a machine-gun destroyer. You would still have to subdue enemy artillery with your own fire, but my bus will get the soldiers across no man's land, through the wire and enable them to deal with the enemy machine-gunners.'

Sir Rufus seemed highly amused. His great body shook with silent laughter.

He said to Hawker senior, 'You know, Hawker, this lad of yours has certainly got a head on his shoulders.' Turning again to Hawker he added: 'I'll tell you what, young fellow, you say you've got a week's leave. If you're able to get yourself up to Suffolk on Thursday morning, you'll maybe see something of great interest to you.'

Sir Rufus called to a waiter and had notepaper brought to the table. With it he wrote Hawker a short letter of

135

introduction and handed it over. He elaborated no further on what the *something of great interest* might be, and flatly refused to be drawn any further on the subject. Instead he pressed Hawker for stories of his flying in France.

Hawker recounted his adventures in a humorous and self-depreciating way and Sir Rufus replied with his own sporting anecdotes. Then Hawker senior, to his son's unfailing delight, ended by relating again the great occasion at Hendon Aerodrome in 1913, when the Frenchman, Adolphe Pégoud, demonstrated the possibility of inverted flight by looping the loop. And at the Royal Automobile Club's celebratory dinner, the meal was served to an 'inverted' menu – starting with the cheese and ending with the soup – and the entertainer, Charles Coburn, brought the evening to a triumphant conclusion by singing 'Two Lovely Black Eyes' standing on his head!

17

Charlie Wren stood in the street eating fish and chips from the paper and looked up the hill at the lights of Blaney Hall, the family home of Captain Lord Rupert Lovell.

After spending the night at his sister's home in London, Wren had gone by bus and tube to St Pancras Station and taken a train north. He had plenty of time on the four-hour journey to consider what had to be done. Hawker had said that a criminal suspect needed opportunity and motive. Wren suspected Captain Lovell. He therefore needed to check out Lovell's background and the only place to do this was in the Lovell heartland, where the family was well known.

He had arrived in Blaney, Yorkshire, at 6.00 p.m. As he strode up the hill from the station, relishing the exercise after the cramped confines of the railway carriage, the shops were beginning to close. In Market Street the butcher, baker and greengrocer already had one shutter up and the workers were clearing away.

There was a chill in the air and a fine drizzle falling. Light from the shopfronts and street lamps shone balefully on the damp cobbles. Wren was famished. At the baker's he rescued a cold meat and potato pie from the almost-bare shelves and wolfed it as he walked along. As Market Street became High Street, a lighted tram clattered by, leading him into the main square. Here the occasional gas lamps gave way to tall electric street lights and the blazing windows of the Town Hall shone with civic pride over a profusion of flower-beds and fountains.

Leaving the square and starting uphill again he came across a fish and chip shop, irresistible in its aromatic pool of light. He ordered cod and chips 'open' and stood for a moment outside, getting his bearings and matching them with the view he'd had from the slowing train and information casually gleaned in the Station Tavern.

Blaney was a typical small Yorkshire town set in a stark, northern landscape embellished by mills and pitheads and overshadowed by great black mountains of slag. Like all towns built on a hill, the further you climbed, the bigger the houses became. Between the station and the square he had passed row upon row of tiny, red-brick cottages, caked with grime from the railway and gasworks. Here, just above the square, the streets were fractionally wider and were lined with end to end workmen's houses – still red-brick, still grimy, but definitely bigger, and more befitting the families of the craftsmen and gaffers that occupied them. Higher still would be the railed terraces and detached residences of the employers and professionals. On top of the heap, overlooking everything, could be seen the aloof, lighted windows of Blaney Hall.

Wren started walking again, eating as he went. He passed a Victorian school building, dark and silent. Above its ornate doorway was an inscription in bold letters, with quotation marks to give it learning: "COME UNTO ME YE CHILDREN I WILL TEACH YOU THE FEAR OF THE LORD".

Wren snorted with amusement and walked on. Moving from street to street he noticed that one in three dwellings had the blinds drawn. Small groups of women gathered in doorways and beneath street lamps. Children milled about and hung on their aprons but there was an air of melancholy and an unnatural quiet. The groups fell silent at Wren's approach and their white eyes searched his face and strange uniform. He nodded silently to them and passed by. Here and there was the light of a corner shop and there were also pubs – lots of pubs. At the first of these he stopped to finish his fish, wiped his hands on the newspaper wrapping and tossed the screwed remnants into a nearby bin. He wiped his face with a handkerchief, straightened his cap and pushed open the door.

He went from pub to pub having a pint in each, chatting to bar staff and asking questions. Being in uniform helped. People, especially women were fascinated by the fact that he was a flyer. Wren chatted easily in a light-hearted way, but he knew he had to find someone who also needed to speak to *him*, who would talk to him freely as a friend. He was prepared to spend most of his week's leave in his task and was just as happy drinking in Blaney as in London – it was cheaper. But Blaney was a small town and after two hours he got his piece of luck.

A barman he spoke to knew a soldier, Sergeant Daniel Tate of the Blaney Pals, who had lost a leg and was invalided home just before the big attack. Tate did his drinking at the Blaney Arms Hotel. He was sweet on the landlady there: a young woman recently widowed when her sailor husband was lost on the *Queen Mary* at Jutland. It was just the break Wren was looking for and he immediately made his way to the Blaney Arms Hotel.

The pretty woman behind the bar wore a sober black dress, jet earrings. and a wedding ring. Wren guessed she was the sailor's widow. He enquired after Sergeant Tate and the woman indicated with a nod of her head a short, thick-set man, sitting alone at a table in the residents' lounge.

Wren made a point of engaging the woman in loud, cheery conversation, turning on the charm and making her laugh, while the man at the table turned repeatedly in his seat and regarded him with mounting hostility. Finally, Wren went over, pulled out a chair and sat down at Tate's table

'Yes?' the man said.

'My name's Wren. I'd like a chat if you don't mind.'

'Why would I want a chat with you?' the man replied belligerently.

Wren played his trump card.

'I was with the Blaney Pals the night before they went over the top.'

The man considered this for a moment then nodded agreement.

'All right. What did you say your name was?'

'Wren. Charlie Wren.'

The man extended his hand.

'Hello Charlie. Daniel Tate. Let's have a drink.' He called to the woman behind the bar: 'Alice!' then turned to Wren: 'What'll it be?'

'A pint,' Wren said. 'Bitter.'

'Two bitters, Alice. And two whiskies.' Tate grinned and winked at Wren. 'Just to get started.' He nodded at Wren's observer brevet. 'What's that, Flying Corps?'

Wren nodded.

'So what were you doing in the line with the Pals, Charlie?'

'We were on a special job, a raid – of sorts,' Wren said.

'And you were with the Pals the night before the attack?'

Wren nodded.

'And afterwards. With what was left of them.'

'So what went wrong,' Tate said.

The landlady brought their drinks on a tray and Wren took advantage of the break to marshal his thoughts. He lit a cigarette, inhaled deeply and exhaled through his nostrils. He took a pull on his pint then screwed up his eyes and looked levelly at Tate through the smoke.

140

'You know the score, Daniel,' he said slowly. 'In this war the success of any attack depends on the artillery killing as many front line defenders as possible and pinning the rest in their dugouts until the attacking infantry can get to them and bomb them out. It was the same at Wipers; the same at Loos. On the Somme, the plan was to step up the barrage and kill all the Huns outright. Then the infantry could take their time and go across all tooled up to face the counter-attacks.'

'But they say none of our boys got anywhere near the Hun front line,' Tate said.

'That's right,' Wren said. 'None that I saw made it more than half-way.'

'You saw them?' Tate said quickly.

'Yes. I helped bring some of the wounded in.'

'You're not a bandsman,' Tate said suspiciously.

In action, army bandsmen doubled as stretcher-bearers.

'No,' Wren said mildly. 'But they needed all the help they could get. They called for volunteers,' he added, laying it on thick.

Tate looked at him for a long moment, then he cleared his throat noisily and busied himself with lighting his pipe.

'You're a good man, Charlie,' he said gruffly.

Wren laughed.

'Right,' he said, draining his glass. 'And a good man always stands his round.' He called to the woman at the bar, 'Two more of the same please, love!'

'So what went wrong?' Tate prompted again.

Wren shrugged.

'Somebody forgot to tell the Huns the plan. Windy bastards stayed down in their dugouts until the barrage lifted. Then they came up and cut our boys down like corn.'

'But the barrage was tremendous, Charlie,' Tate exclaimed. 'It went on for seven days and nights. It was the biggest barrage put down by any army anywhere!'

141

'It still wasn't enough,' Wren said impassively. 'The Huns were 40 feet underground. And we'd so conned ourselves into believing the barrage would do its job, we didn't consider what would happen if it didn't.'

'But we *all* believed it, Charlie. How could the whole crowd of us have been so wrong?' Tate demanded.

To Wren, the answer came all to easily. Roy the magician had been right. *To measure the intelligence of a crowd, you don't multiply by the number of people – you divide. And it's not difficult to fool people when they want to be fooled.* The words were on the tip of his tongue, but he couldn't say them. Not to this man.

'We all *wanted* to believe it,' he said finally. 'Anyone who thought differently felt they were letting the side down. So we kept quiet. The *main* thing was the failure of the barrage. The Hawthorn mine going up early didn't help matters and there were other local disasters all along the front. As soon as the attack started the people in the first wave knew that it had failed. But there was so much dust and smoke and shit flying about, the second and third waves didn't know what was going on and they just kept moving forward.'

'I can't believe it,' Daniel said wonderingly, his eyes filling up. 'All those young lads. What rotten, bastard luck!'

'It was more than that,' Wren said severely, thinking that if any of them put it down to just bad luck – even in their own minds – then the same stupid mistakes could be made all over again.

He stopped talking as Alice, the landlady, brought the second round of drinks and stood beside their table.

'Are you gentlemen dining?' she asked with mock ceremony.

'You know *I* am,' Tate replied. 'What about you, Charlie? You might as well, you won't get better around here.'

'I don't know,' Wren said. 'First I've got to find a bed for the night. I've got no digs.'

'How about it, Alice,' Tate said. 'Any vacancies?'

Alice nodded to Wren.

'Yes, we can fix you up.'

'All right,' Wren said. 'I'll eat then.' He grinned up at Alice. 'What's the special?'

'There's nothing special,' Alice replied curtly. 'There's beef and onion pie and apple pie to follow. Take it or leave it.'

'He'll take it,' Tate said soothingly. He winked at Wren. 'Alice's apple pies *are* special, Charlie. And plenty of cheese on top.' He said to Alice.

'What on top?' Wren demanded.

'Cheese, lad,' Tate said. 'You can't have apple pie without the cheese!'

'Apple without the cheese; is like a kiss without the squeeze,' Alice chanted, smiling at Wren.

'If you say so,' Wren said doubtfully. 'All right. I'll have beef pie and apple pie – with cheese.'

Alice curtsied sarcastically and returned to the bar.

'You like your pastry up here,' Wren commented.

'Needs must, Charlie,' Tate replied. 'Folk up north can't afford much meat. Pastry pads it out a bit.' He applied a match to his pipe, which had gone out. 'Our problem, Charlie, is that all the money is made in the north and spent in the south.'

'Where's your violin?' Wren replied drily. Then he saw his cue. 'Some of you do all right.'

'Meaning what?' Tate said.

'That big house up on the hill, for instance. The people who live up there must have a few bob.'

'That's Blaney Hall,' Tate said matter-of-factly. 'Lord Blaney's place.'

'I know,' Wren said.

Tate shook his head and frowned irritably.

'So what are you getting at?'

143

Wren grinned and took his time lighting another cigarette.

Finally he said, 'I'd like you to tell me something, Daniel. If you want to that is.'

Tate shrugged. 'What is it you want to know?'

'I said earlier that we were in the Pals' sector because we were there to carry out a raid.'

Tate nodded.

Wren watched him closely. 'The raid was led by Captain Rupert Lovell.'

Tate was tapping his pipe out in the ashtray. He looked up in surprise.

'*Lord* Lovell? Lord Blaney's son?'

'That's right,' Wren said. 'D'you know him?'

Tate frowned.

'Not personally, no. But everyone around here knows the Lovell family. Lord Blaney is the local landowner. He owns all the land and he's got an interest in all the mines and mills.' Tate shrugged and looked around him. 'You could say he owns the town and all the people in it. We know him all right!'

'The family's rich then?' Wren said.

Tate nodded thoughtfully.

'Rich? Yes. At least, you'd think so.'

He refilled his pipe and took a while lighting up again. Clouds of smoke billowed across the room.

Alice at the bar coughed involuntarily and waved her hand before her face.

'That blasted pipe, Daniel. Spare a thought for other people!'

'There's now't wrong with pipe tobacco,' Daniel said contentedly, blowing out the match. 'It soothes the nerves and kills the germs.'

'It gets on *my* nerves and will more likely kill the customers,' Alice retorted hotly.

144

She made a great show of rushing to a window, opening the sash a crack and flouncing back to the bar. She gave Wren a glance as she passed and he guessed she was showing off for his benefit. He winked and grinned at her.

Wren nodded at Alice's retreating back.

'Have you got ambitions in that direction, Daniel?' he asked quietly.

'Me and Alice?' Tate said, and nodded seriously. 'In time. There's no sense in rushing anything. She's only been widowed five weeks. But she can't manage this place on her own. I've got a bit of property myself and a pension for this.' He tapped his wooden leg with his walking stick. 'We'll get together when the time's right.'

'You live here? Wren asked.

''Course not!' Tate looked shocked. ' I couldn't live in. It wouldn't look right. We'll get together in time.'

Wren thought of how the woman had looked at him.

'Don't leave it too long,' he warned.

Both men sipped their whisky and took long pulls at their pints.

'I was saying,' Tate went on, and pointed with his pipe. 'You'd *think* the Lovells were rich. You might or might not be right.'

'What d'you mean?' Wren said impatiently.

Not for the first time, he thought that northerners preferred to talk in riddles just to get your attention.

Tate looked carefully at all the drinkers sitting around the bar, then leaned across the table and lowered his voice.

'Well, they've still got the land. No doubt of that. And they've still got the house. But big houses cost big money to run. And from what I hear, the family's a little bit short of the readies. They've got no cash!'

He sat back triumphantly.

'How come?' Wren asked.

'Well,' Tate explained, 'Lord Blaney, the old man, has

145

been a bit funny in the head for years now. That's common knowledge. But recently, they say, he's got worse. He's been giving money away. Bloody throwing it about. Thousands of pounds to charity – so called "good causes". Anything to do with animals: the PDSA and such-like. And anything to do with fallen women. They were the things guaranteed to make him stump up.' Tate grinned. 'Guilty conscience if you ask me. Of course, as the word got round, requests for donations started to come from all directions – some real, some bogus. I even heard that two of the gardeners up at the Hall got together and founded a few charities of their own. They had notepaper done with highfalutin' titles and used a relative's address. They got found out and lost their jobs but no charges were brought. The family wanted it kept quiet.'

'Where did you hear all this?' Wren asked doubtfully.

Tate looked around carefully again.

'My cousin Polly is a maid up at the Hall,' he whispered. 'It's not just gossip, Charlie. Polly's not like that. It's the truth all right.'

'Is it commonly known?' Wren asked.

Tate shook his head.

'Not commonly. Of course, quite a few people know about it but they're careful about what they say. The Lovells are very powerful around here. It wouldn't do to get on the wrong side of them. People wouldn't normally talk about it. I'm telling you because you were with the Pals.' He grinned ironically. 'And because I like you. But they say that things have got so bad that the family have had to have the old boy committed.'

'Committed?' Wren said.

'Legally committed to an institution,' Tate explained patiently. 'Put in a loony bin. Banged up in the big house. It was the only way they could stop him giving away the family cash.' Daniel snorted ironically. 'The joke is, the old

146

man is in Rebecca House, the mental institution he built for the town twenty years ago. Named it after his missus, Lady Blaney, who also went doolally before she died. I'll bet the old boy never thought he'd wind up in there himself!'

'What's Lord Lovell, the son, like?' Wren asked.

'What's he like?' Tate replied with a laugh. 'Why, he's as mad as a hatter, always has been! First sons of the nobility, Charlie, are always wild men. Because they know that when they succeed to the title, their life won't be their own any more. Once they become the Earl, they have to get married, sire an heir and maintain the family seat until they die. And if the family's not rolling in loot it'll be a nightmare.'

'So what do you reckon Lovell, the son, will do if they're skint like you say?' Wren said.

'He'll get money somehow,' Tate said. 'He's a canny bugger. I reckon he'll go back to India after the war. They're always having little local wars out there. It wouldn't be difficult for someone with Lovell's influence to stir up trouble and get his hands on some loot.'

Wren looked at Tate and shook his head dubiously.

'I dunno, ' he said, 'This war won't be over for a while yet. It mightn't be that easy.'

'He'll get it somehow,' Tate asserted. 'Ever since he was a little lad, it's been drummed into him that he's just a link in an aristocratic chain and his great duty in life is the continuation of the family name and estate. Mark my words, Charlie. He'll get the money. No matter what it takes!'

Somewhere in the town a church clock struck one. Charlie Wren settled himself comfortably in the big bed. He had bought a half-bottle of whisky over the bar and swigged it contentedly as he thought over the day's events. In particular, he considered the information about the Lovell family gleaned from Daniel Tate. This knowledge turned the

147

mystery of the missing jewels on its head and demolished, at a stroke, half of Hawker's argument in the Captain's defence. Wren's eyelids began to droop and he acknowledged reluctantly that the hour was too late for careful thought. It had been a long day. He took a final swig of his bottle and was about to turn out the light when there was a sudden knock on his door.

'Come in,' Wren said.

It was Alice, the landlady. She was in her dressing gown.

'I saw the light,' she said. 'Everything all right?'

'Fine, thanks,' Wren said.

'Got everything you want?'

'Not everything,' Wren grinned.

Alice smiled faintly. 'What is it you want?'

'Tender loving care,' Wren said.

'We all want that,' Alice said matter-of-factly. Then she added, 'My husband was lost at sea. He was on the *Queen Mary* at Jutland.'

'I know,' Wren said gently. He picked up his whisky bottle again. 'Come and have a drink,' he said.

Alice closed the door and came and sat on the bed. She was shivering. Wren took a drink from the bottle and passed it to her. Alice up-ended it briefly, made a face and shuddered. She handed the bottle back. She was still shivering.

Wren moved over in the bed and turned back the bedclothes.

'Get in,' he said. 'You'll catch cold.'

Alice got in. She was still wearing her dressing gown.

Wren switched out the light and moved towards her. She shivered again at his touch and he hesitated.

'Are you all right?' he asked softly.

She nodded against his cheek.

'Hold me,' she said.

Wren woke once in the night. Alice was sound asleep and he went to the window and stared out at the sleeping town.

Everywhere, across and down the hill, lights glimmered in the houses and cottages where sleepless families made tea through the small hours and thought of the men who had gone away and now slept forever in a foreign place called Serre.

On the second day of the big attack, Wren had crossed no man's land, and walked through the copses behind the Blaney Pals' front line. The whole area was thick with dead, dying and wounded. Hundreds of stretcher cases waited in rows for their turn to be moved to casualty stations in the rear. Some moaned, some cried out, but mostly they lay in resigned silence, tended by weary, overstretched doctors and orderlies. All too often, their turn came too late, and after cursory inspection by an MO, they were taken away for swift burial in mass graves.

Kitchener's young army had paid a hard price for its first lesson in war. But Wren knew that the true, enduring cost of the Somme battle was being paid here, in a small northern town, and in a thousand other towns and villages across the country.

18

Hawker stood rooted to the spot and his mind reeled as he struggled to rationalise the sight before him. For a moment he was completely disorientated and, doubting the evidence of his own eyes, spun on his heel to stare wildly at the calm English countryside behind. Then, reassured of his sanity, he turned once more to the astonishing scene.

After spending Tuesday night at the Royal Automobile Club, Hawker had travelled with his father to their family home in Bedfordshire. But he had been intrigued by Sir Rufus Strong's invitation. That same afternoon, ignoring his mother's protests, he had got his old motorcycle out of the garage and had ridden up to Thetford on the Norfolk/Suffolk border. He spent the night at The Bell Hotel in the town, and was up bright and early on Thursday morning to ride the few miles to Lord Iveagh's Elveden Estate.

The spartan heath and woodland was empty of habitation except for a few farms but, just past Elveden village, canvas screens lined the main Thetford-Newmarket road and there was a profusion of notices announcing: ELVEDEN EXPLOSIVES AREA – KEEP OUT! At every hundred yards Hawker had to stop to show Sir Rufus's letter and proof of identity to Royal Defence Corps sentries. Finally, he entered the grounds by a heavily-guarded farm gate, parked his motorcycle and followed a pathway through the trees. As he emerged from the trees, the path led to a high man-made bank, surmounted by a timber viewing platform. Hawker climbed the platform steps and was confronted by the most amazing spectacle he had ever seen.

On the area of land before him, army engineers had carved out a replica battlefield. Opposing front lines of concrete emplacements, trenches and barbed wire faced each other over an authentic belt of no man's land complete with shell holes and stonework 'ruins'; and littered with blasted tree trunks, wrecked vehicles and assorted debris. Intermittent explosions erupted spewing mud and steam, and machine-gun tracer flickered back and forth. Yet it wasn't the sights and sounds of war in this quiet corner of England that caused Hawker to gape like a fool, shamble to the edge of the platform and grip the wooden guard rail like a man in a dream.

Roaming this forlorn moonscape were dozens of huge, iron-clad cars. They must be cars because the air was filled with the roar of heavy motors and blue petrol fumes mingled in the air with the blast and steam and smoke of battle. They crawled on twin steel tracks but, unlike the Holts tractors already employed in France, these caterpillars ran around the entire body of the vehicle. No wheels or working parts were visible and every surface was covered with armour plate. The profile was of a drunken rectangle or rhomboid, leaning forward so that the tracks at the front could easily breast and surmount obstacles. Hawker shook his head in admiration. The shape was both functional and futuristic. It could have been a piece of shipyard scrap or a Martian invasion vehicle.

'They're called "tanks".'

Hawker turned at the voice behind him and saw a young officer approaching, hand outstretched in greeting.

'Lieutenant Hawker?' the newcomer asked, smiling.

'Yes.'

'Lieutenant Sampson, 'D' Company, Heavy Section,

151

Machine Gun Corps. The CO sent me along to explain what we're doing here.' He nodded at the war scene before them. 'Pretty impressive isn't it.'

'It's absolutely amazing!' Hawker agreed, shaking his head in wonder. He continued to stare wide-eyed as Lieutenant Sampson proudly described the new vehicles' specifications and abilities.

Each tank weighed 27 tons and was powered by a Daimler six-cylinder 105 hp petrol engine. It was 26 feet long, 14 feet wide and 8 feet high. It could climb a one-in-three slope, cross a six-foot trench and crawl in 30 inches of water. The armour could withstand machine guns and shrapnel but not a direct hit by artillery. Top speed – downhill and with a following wind – was three-and-half miles per hour.

For some reason, a tank was known officially as a 'landship' and the naval terminology extended to calling the front the 'prow', the rear the 'stern' and the men manning it the 'crew'. Each vehicle carried a crew of eight: a commander and driver in the forward turret; four gunners in the side-sponsons; and two 'gearsmen' to help the driver work the engine and gears.

Astonishingly, there were two species of tank: male and female. Both had sponsons – metal turrets bolted each side of the hull – but while the 'males' carried two six-pounder naval guns to engage enemy machine-guns and concrete emplacements, the 'females' mounted four Vickers guns to catch and punish Hun infantry.

'My tank is a female,' Lieutenant Sampson added affectionately.

'What do you call her?' Hawker asked.

Sampson grinned sheepishly. *Delilah*,' he said. 'What else?'

Hawker's delighted laughter was drowned as a formation of three tanks passed directly in front of them. One of the monsters broke away and turned towards the platform. It

152

came straight towards them rearing and lurching until Hawker could see the driver's viewing ports and individual rivets on the armour plate. It advanced alarmingly until the tracks were only a couple of feet from the platform; then it stopped abruptly, revving and roaring in a cloud of exhaust fumes.

From their raised vantage point they could see over the front turret to a circular manhole in the vehicle's roof. As they watched, the hatch opened and a figure emerged; an alien figure in overalls and leather helmet, the face obscured by metal goggles and a mask of chain-mail. It strode confidently along the roof of the tank crossed the bridge of the extended tracks, grasped the wooden rail and vaulted over. For a moment the stranger stood silently before them. Then, with a theatrical flourish he removed his helmet and mask and Hawker stared into the grinning face of Captain Lord Rupert Lovell.

Charlie Wren's night with the woman had done him good. It had relaxed him and restored his strength and confidence. Returning on the London train, he again addressed himself to the problem of the missing jewels.

Wren had never really believed Jacko Bass was guilty. And yet it had seemed inconceiveable that Captain Lovell himself was the thief. Hawker had said that a suspect must be shown to have had motive and opportunity. Initially, it seemed that the heir to the Blaney estates could *have* no motive, but Wren's quest in the north had disproved this: the family needed cash. But what of opportunity? The sequence of events surrounding the jewels' disappearance also seemed, on the face of it, to preclude Lovell as a suspect.

Wren sat in the carriage of the south-bound train, smoking intently and going step by step over the events that led to the disappearance of the jewels. In his mind was the phrase which first planted the seed of doubt; the words uttered by Roy the magician: *When something disappears, it has to go somewhere else. And if that seems impossible, then perhaps it wasn't where you thought it was in the first place!*

The train took four-and-a-half hours to reach London but when it pulled into St Pancras Wren was convinced he knew the answer. If he was right, Captain Lovell had motive *and* opportunity. He *must* be guilty.

19

'Right, pay attention. This is the plan.'

Captain Lovell, with his back to the tent-wall, tapped with a swagger stick on the large map easel beside him. Facing him were his tank crew: Hawker the driver; four Vicker's machine-gunners – Charlie Wren, Sergeant Pidgeon, Gunners Large and Small; and the two gearsmen – Gunners Green and Black. They watched him intently, for their joint fortunes in the coming battle depended on what he had to say.

After his meeting with Captain Lovell at Elveden, Hawker had stayed at the tank depot for a further four weeks. Lovell had declared himself to be still on the trail of the missing jewels and he was sure that he knew where the fugitive Private Bass had hidden them. Furthermore, he had convinced the powers that be that there was a real chance of recovering the treasure; and they had allowed him to join the new tank force that was shortly to be used in an attack on the German line at Flers.

Lovell also wanted Sergeant Wren to be in on it ('All of the old firm,' Lovell had said, laughing). Wren had been duly sent for and the three had been allocated a tank and crew, and had trained with the rest of 'D' Company, Heavy Section, Machine Gun Corps – the cover name of the new mechanised force.

Hawker was thrilled with his new posting and gleefully 'bagged' the job of tank driver.

Wren was less enthusiastic. He didn't believe Lovell could know where Jacko had hidden the loot and he voiced his reservations to Hawker.

Hawker frowned his concern.

'Charlie, are you still harbouring doubts about Captain Lovell's honesty?'

'Since you mention it, sir,' Wren said drily.

'But if there was anything funny about what happened at Flers the last time, why would the captain want us around again?'

'I don't know, sir, Wren replied. 'Perhaps he thinks we were easy to fool before, and will be again.'

And there was another thing. Wren had noticed that Captain Lovell was wearing a black arm band on the left sleeve of his tunic. He asked Hawker what it was for.

Hawker shook his head solemnly.

'A very sad business, Charlie. Captain Lovell's father died recently. The captain's very cut up about it. He's also very mindful of his new responsibilities. Because, of course, Captain Lovell is now the seventh Earl of Blaney.'

On 2 September, 'D' Company tanks had been taken by rail to Avonmouth and across the Channel to Le Havre. They travelled on the French railway system to a secret depot near Yvrench village, north-east of Abbeville. After another week's training they were again loaded onto railway trucks for the journey to 'Happy Valley', midway between the villages of Bray-sur-Somme and Mametz. It was here that Lovell outlined the plan.

Pinned to his map easel was a large-scale British War Department map showing three French villages and the roads linking them. The configuration resembled a tall, mis-shapen pyramid. The peak of the pyramid, was the village of Flers; and the base was formed by the road linking the

156

villages of Longueval on the left and Ginchy on the right. Between the villages and all around, was a puzzle of solid and broken lines showing every British and enemy trench in the area.

'This afternoon,' Lovell continued, 'we move from here and take up our final positions on the start line for the big attack. On the day after next, the morning of the fifteenth of September, we, together with other tanks of 'D' Company and infantry of the 14th, 41st, New Zealand and Guards Divisions will attack German positions defending the village of Flers.

'The British front line is the trench called Pilsen Lane which runs along the northern edge of the Longueval-Ginchy Road. We will be here.' Lovell indicated a point just south of the road and roughly central between the two villages. 'To our left: Delville Wood, unsuitable for tanks as all the trees have been flattened by shell-fire and the ground is littered with stumps and severed branches. Ahead and to our right: the Brewery Salient, so named for obvious reasons and still occupied by the enemy. They hold strong positions in Hop Alley, Ale Alley, and in Beer Trench and Pint Trench. It is thought that these forward Hun positions could break down the main assault before it gets under way; so at 5.10 a.m., prior to the main attack, two tanks: *Daredevil* and *Dolphin* will go forward to clear the Brewery Salient.

'You won't be surprised to hear,' Lovell continued, 'that, besides our special mission, we also have an important role in the main attack.' Lovell pointed with his stick at Flers village. 'In the centre of Flers, on the left just before the church, is the entrance to a communication tunnel.' He grinned ironically. 'Lieutenant Hawker and Sergeant Wren already know it well. It's deep underground and emerges here, on the north-west edge of the village close to the l'Abbaye d'Eaucourt road. When the the southern half of the village is taken, our job will be to block the tunnel

entrance near the church and prevent German reinforcements emerging behind the line of attack. We also have to
cover the main street in the event of the enemy counter-
attacking through the village.'

Lovell nodded grimly and looked at all of them in turn.

'Ours is a vital role. As they move to secure the northern
half of the village, our people must be sure that no Huns
can get through the tunnel or down the main street.'

'Any questions?' Lovell asked finally. When there were
none he continued. 'Now,' he said breezily, 'we have one
more vital thing to do. Every ship must have a name; even a
land-ship. What will it be? Remember, she's female, completely deaf, almost blind and absolutely terrifying!'

'Sounds like my Great-aunt Mavis,' Hawker quipped.

Lovell guffawed and then frowned thoughtfully.

'We had a hunting mare named Mavis. Never refused a
fence in her life.' He nodded decisively. 'It's a good name;
HMLS *Mavis* it is!'

'Excuse me, sir,' Sergeant Pidgeon put in firmly. 'This is
a 'D' Company tank. 'D' Company tanks have names beginning with D.'

'Nonsense!' Lovell retorted. '*Mavis* isn't with 'D' Company. She's on independent, special duty.'

'Just as you say, sir,' Pidgeon said stonily and turned away.

'Lieutenant Hawker,' Lovell ordered. 'Get *Mavis*'s name
painted on her prow.'

Certainly, sir,' Hawker said happily. 'Sergeant Wren, get
the tank's name painted up.'

'Right, sir,' Wren said. 'Gunner Green, fetch a pot of
white paint and christen the tank.'

'Okay, Sarge,' Green replied wearily. And as he trudged
off to stores, he muttered to himself, 'What a load of balls!'

*

That afternoon, 'D' Company tanks drove under their own power to their start points for the attack. The journey took them the rest of the day, for they drove in bottom gear at less than a mile an hour. They moved in convoy at first, but later, as they approached their individual destinations, they turned off one by one to go their separate ways.

Throughout this journey Hawker was in his element as he jockeyed *Mavis* over every kind of ground and obstacle: nursing the throttle, jerking the wheel to keep her straight and slipping the clutch to stop her stalling. It was an ideal test of his skills, albeit in favourable conditions.

Their passage up to the lines was greeted with awe by the astonished infantrymen. Every yard of their progress through the back areas was followed by crowds of off-duty troops who followed along beside them staring in disbelief. Then, with broad grins replacing the original looks of wonder, they began to place various pieces of rubbish in the monster's way: discarded petrol tins; defunct road signs; German helmets. *Mavis* dutifully crushed them all flat beneath her tracks and each demolition was greeted by a great cheer from the delighted Tommies.

Daredevil and *Mavis* had the farthest to go and they finally reached their destination in the early hours of 14 September. The crews were exhausted and, rolling blankets beside the tanks, they fell instantly asleep.

The day was spent preparing for the attack. After their journey, the tanks needed a full service. Engines had to be retuned; tracks tightened; every moving part oiled or greased. Weapons were checked; ammunition loaded; iron rations, water and spare cans of petrol stowed and secured.

Training in England and at camps in France, the tank-men had fancied themselves as they swaggered in their leather helmets with pistols on their belts. But all that was forgotten. Now they had to lead into no man's land in their

159

untried machines, each one of them a prime target for prepared artillery. There was an air of tension, for they knew that if they or their machines were found wanting, they could expect no quarter from the enemy or sympathy from their own infantry who expected so much of them.

As the day ended, Lovell and his crew finally rolled themselves in their blankets and tried to rest. Sleep was impossible. All through the night, behind and on each side, infantry were marching forward, taking up their attack positions. Overhead, the scream of shells steadily increased as the barrage fell on the German front line.

Then, at 4.45 a.m., a messenger came from Brigade to tell them the plan had been changed. HMLS *Dolphin*, had got into difficulties circumventing Delville Wood and would not arrive on time to partner *Daredevil. Mavis* must therefore go forward at 5.10 a.m. to support *Daredevil* in the preliminary assault on the Brewery Salient.

Lovell was outraged at this interference in his private war. *Mavis* could easily be disabled in this added task and their mission could be washed out before it started. His rousing of the crew was therefore none too gentle and everyone climbed aboard feeling resentful and uneasy.

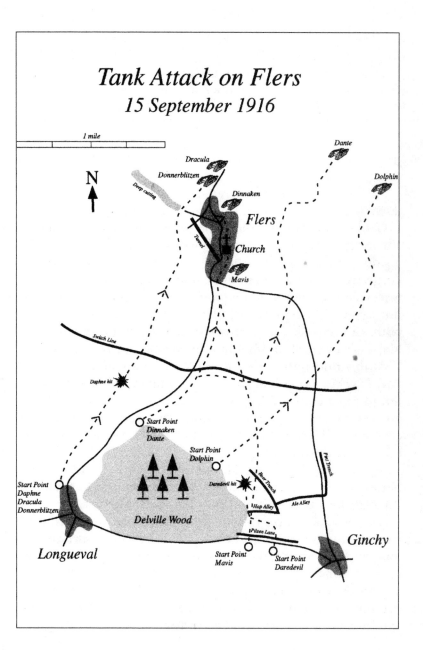

Tank Attack on Flers
15 September 1916

1 mile

N

Dracula

Donnerblitzen

Deep cutting

Dinnaken

Dante

Dolphin

Flers

Tunnel

Church

Mavis

Switch Line

Daphne hit

Start Point
Dinnaken
Dante

Start Point
Dolphin

Daredevil hit

Beer Trench

Pot Trench

Start Point
Daphne
Dracula
Donnerblitzen

Hop Alley

Ale Alley

Delville Wood

Pilsen Lane

Ginchy

Longueval

Start Point
Mavis

Start Point
Daredevil

20

'Forward!'

Captain Lovell mouthed the word silently and pointed ahead through the prisms of his closed front port. The din inside the iron body of the tank required all commands to be given in mime. Hawker turned in his seat and banged twice on the engine casing with a big spanner. When the two gearsmen looked up from their controls, Hawker pointed forward. The gearsmen threw their levers and His Majesty's Land Ship *Mavis* lumbered into no man's land.

At this hour, beneath the horizon, it was still dark. Lovell and Hawker both opened their front ports but it was still no good; they couldn't see a thing. Earlier, they had been guided across the British front line trenches by guides carrying luminous discs. Now they had been left on their own to rendezvous with *Daredevil.*

Lovell climbed out of the main hatch in the roof to get a better view. A few minutes later he returned, squinted through his open port and shouted in Hawker's ear.

'*Daredevil* is just off to our right. He's crossing in front of us. When you see him, just follow on behind. *Daredevil* is a male tank. I don't want to risk getting in the way of one of his six-pounders.'

Hawker stuck up a thumb in acknowledgment and they rumbled on. The noise inside the tank was terrific. The 105 hp petrol engine, linked through three separate gearboxes, drove two caterpillar tracks which ran on cogs and drive-wheels around the external skin of the vehicle. In the metal sound-box of the hull, the crew sweated in the din and heat and fumes from the engine. They wore full standard uniform and were further encumbered by leather helmets, goggles and chain-mail face masks. Seen through the blue leaking fumes and lit by the sparse glimmer of electric lights, they looked like beings from another planet toiling in a cavern of hell.

It was 5.45 a.m. For the first time, the surrounding terrain became discernible in a pre-dawn half-light. Hawker's feet no longer hovered uncertainly over clutch and brake as *Mavis* plunged into unseen pits and breasted invisible obstacles. Now he drove her confidently over the grey but solid terrain, while the rest of the crew braced themselves more confidently and peered curiously through their viewing slits for their first sight of the enemy.

Gunners cocked their pieces and swung their weapons looking for targets. The four Vickers machine-guns each swung through 45 degrees and could, in theory, cover a target positioned at any of the 360 degrees around the tank. But tank gunners knew that to fire effectively while on the move was next to impossible. Gunners crouched at their weapon seated on a polished wood stool attached to the gun. To preserve the vehicle's armoured integrity, the slit that the guns fired through (also extending through 45 degrees) had to be masked by a bullet-proof shield mounted inside and swung with the gun. Seeking targets through a tiny aperture and the smoke and dust of battle, the gunners had to swing the combined weight of gun, mounting, seat and shield; and all the while they and their weapons were moving forward, lurching to left and right; diving or climbing over the terrain and debris of no man's land.

So tank gunners saved their ammunition and waited for

the *great day*. The tank had been conceived to overcome trenches and machine-gun emplacements. The *great day* would come when they sat astride an enemy front-line trench, crushing a Maxim gun and its crew beneath their tracks, with every gunner blazing away at the helpless Huns fleeing to the rear.

Lovell pointed ahead and Hawker could see the dark bulk of *Daredevil* crossing in front, heading for the edge of Delville Wood. Hawker followed him. He could clearly see the sponsons on each side and the six-pounder guns swinging in search of targets. There was a sudden flash as the port gun fired into the wood.

Hawker cheered excitedly.

'Go it *Daredevil*!'

Flashes of fire flickered along the edge of the wood and off to the right as the Germans in Hop Alley and Ale Alley returned fire. There came a rattling on *Mavis's* hull; the sound was exactly that of pebbles falling on a corrugated iron roof. Lovell and Hawker looked at each other and grinned. The feeling of immunity was delicious.

Lovell grabbed the pistol grip of the forward-firing Hotchkiss and loosed a whole strip in the direction of Hop Alley. *Daredevil's* six-pounders fired again, and there was a terrific hammering racket as *Mavis's* Vickers guns opened up. The tank was filled with the stink of cordite.

'Give it to them, chaps!' Hawker shouted joyously.

Then, as suddenly as it had begun, the enemy fire ceased. Distant figures emerged from the wood and fled northwards, joining those running from Hop Alley and Ale Alley. *Mavis's* Vickers hammered in pursuit.

'Cease fire!' Lovell yelled. 'Driver, stop!'

Lovell made his way back to the main hatch and climbed out. The rest of the crew rushed to open hatches and let out the choking smoke and fumes. Through the open ports they could see that *Mavis* and *Daredevil* were surrounded by

164

grinning, cheering infantrymen who had followed them from Pilsen Lane and advanced from inside Delville Wood. They were happily taking over the deserted German trenches. It seemed incredible. The Brewery Salient had been cleared in 30 minutes!

Lovell dropped back down inside the tank and grinned at them He rubbed his hands in satisfaction.

'Well done, chaps,' he said. 'Now for Flers!'

The main attack was due to start at 6.20 a.m. As soon as the creeping barrage began to fall ahead of them, the two tanks and the accompanying infantry moved along behind it. Almost immediately, *Daredevil* was hit. Hawker, off to the right and slightly behind, saw a shell burst on the the starboard track. *Daredevil* trundled on but the broken track trailed like entrails in his wake. When the track ran out *Daredevil* was immobile. Some of the crew clambered out to view the damage. Captain Mortimore, the commander, stood on the roof waving *Mavis* on while one of his six-pounders banged in defiance.

Mavis was now leading the infantry alone. Up to now, Lovell and Hawker had been confidently driving with the front ports open. After seeing what had happened to *Daredevil*, they closed up and and braced themselves grimly.

With all hatches closed, the atmosphere inside degenerated rapidly and soon became unbearable. At last Lovell reopened his viewing port and ordered the rear hatch opened. With a through-draught conditions improved, but five minutes later something came through Lovell's port, miraculously missed his head and holed the forward exhaust stack. This began to belch fumes and the air quality deteriorated again.

It was 6.45 a.m. Since starting off they had been travelling slightly downhill, but now the ground began to rise. Hawker halted the tank. He couldn't change gear in the usual fashion as with a motorcycle or car. The tank's weight and slow speed meant that any interruption in drive caused it to come to a dead stop. Whenever there was a change in terrain, Hawker had to stop the tank, decide on the appropriate gear, and signal to the gearsmen.

With engine roaring, *Mavis* attacked the slope. They had now advanced beyond the northern edge of Delville Wood and to their left 'D' Company tanks could be seen advancing, followed by lines of infantry.

One of the gearsmen came forward and tapped Lovell on the shoulder.

Leaning close to Lovell's ear he shouted, 'There's a tank crossing from port to starboard behind us, sir.'

Lovell went back to have a look out of the rear hatch.

'That'll be *Dolphin*,' Lovell shouted. 'Better late than never!'

This slope was the first obstacle of the notorious Switch Line. The Switch was three miles long and guarded Flers and Martinpuich. Its deep, heavily-manned ramparts were guarded by belts of barbed wire and concreted machine-gun posts. Artillery fire from beyond Flers plastered the forward slopes. The Switch line had been attacked continuously throughout the previous July and August but had never been broken.

But in July and August there were no tanks. Now seven of the monsters ground inexorably forward. Lovell identified them through his binoculars. To his right was the solitary *Dolphin*; to his left *Daphne, Dracula, Donnerblitzen, Dinnaken* and *Dante*.

But even as he watched, *Daphne* took a direct hit as a shell exploded full on her forward turret. The crew came tumbling out of the sponson doors. As they tried to run clear of the blazing tank, machine guns firing from the Switch bowled them over like ninepins.

166

Lovell's reaction was to close all hatches. This was the crucial point of the attack; they would have to stick it out. A shell exploded directly in front, showering *Mavis* with earth and debris. Something smashed the prisms of Hawker's viewing port, distorting his vision and throwing glass splinters like needles against his goggles and chain-mail mask. In desperation, he tore off his goggles and threw open the port.

The slope grew steeper and Mavis strained to take it. Her engine note fell and she teetered on the edge of a stall.

'Come on, *Mavis!*' Hawker cried desperately.

Slipping the clutch and gunning the throttle, he gripped the wheel and rocked in his seat to will her forward.

Roaring and grinding, the tank inched upwards. As it breasted the ridge it reared up. The crew braced themselves, hanging on grimly. Machine-gun bullets rattled on the hull. Then, with a teeth-jarring jolt, they crashed back onto an even keel. Simultaneously, the sounds of enemy fire ceased and all four of *Mavis's* Vickers guns began to hammer in long bursts. This was it! They were astride the German front line. The dreaded Switch Line had been breached!

Through their open ports Lovell and Hawker beheld an amazing sight. The downward slope to their front was alive with Germans fleeing towards Flers. Left and right, other tanks perched on the ridge, six-pounders blasting, machine-guns hammering. All around the tanks, British infantry stood or knelt, firing their rifles, working their bolts, exultantly blazing away at the helpless enemy. All their trepidation, worry and fear of the previous days and nights had turned to righteous rage; to an indignant, merciless need to punish and kill.

At last the firing diminished and died away. The only Huns left were dead or wounded. Tanks and infantry began to move down the slope towards Flers. Enemy shells began to fall on the slope and the British barrage turned its attention to Flers itself. Captain Lovell stood on the roof of the tank and peered through his binoculars. Amid the explosions and dust he could just discern the broken but unmistakeable outline of Flers church.

21

'Who's throwing pebbles on my roof?' Captain Lovell roared at the now familiar sound of enemy fire hitting the tank's armoured hull. 'I see you, you bugger! He's in the rafters of the first building on the right. Driver, take down that wall!'

Hawker swung the wheel and the tank gently nudged the wall of the burnt out cottage. It buckled like paper and the building collapsed in a cloud of dust and ashes. *Mavis's* Vickers guns hammered, seeking the enemy who scuttled from the ruins.

'D' Company tanks, followed by cautious groups of infantry, were launching a full-scale assault on Flers village. *Dracula* and *Donnerblitzen* had continued the course that took them up the village's western edge; *Dante* and *Dolphin* had swung right to sweep the eastern outskirts; *Dinnaken* and *Mavis* headed directly into Flers, advancing up the main street.

Lovell opened the hatch in the roof and climbed up to get a better view. As he did so, a lone British aircraft swooped low overhead, rocking its wings in salute. The crowds of infantry following the tanks waved and cheered. But as they rounded the first bend in the road, they encountered renewed enemy resistance. Maxim guns opened up and the infantry took casualties before falling back and going to ground.

Dinnaken, a male tank, forged ahead, his six-pounders

banging left and right. *Mavis*'s Vickers systematically raked the buildings on each side. As she approached the tunnel that was her main objective, the crew again heard the tell-tale sound of enemy fire hitting home. German defenders were still holding out in the tunnel mouth.

For the first time, Lovell's men felt the alarming effects of point blank machine-gun fire hitting the hull face-on. Lumps of molten lead splashed through the crevices between the armour plate; slivers of steel from the inner skin broke away and flew around the crew compartments penetrating clothing and flesh. The tankmen's reaction was to blaze away into the tunnel mouth with every weapon that could be brought to bear. The noise was tremendous as Vickers guns and revolvers hammered and banged. The air was thick with smoke and cordite. Sweating in their helmets and face masks, men cursed as they stumbled over the hundreds of brass cartridge cases piling up on the floor.

Hawker drove *Mavis* right into the tunnel mouth. Lovell fired strip after strip from the commander's Hotchkiss, loosing a stream of lead into the darkness. At last all symptoms of enemy fire vanished.

'Cease fire!' Lovell shouted.

Wielding the Hotchkiss gun, he swung himself out of the rear hatch. Wren followed, drawing his Luger pistol. Lovell raced into the tunnel entrance. He fired a burst into the darkness and there was a single answering shot that sang off the tank's hull. Lovell held the Hotchkiss on his hip and fired a full strip down the tunnel.

Wren smiled grimly. Lovell might be a thieving, murdering bastard but he was a bloody good soldier. This time there was no answering fire and they heard running footsteps as the enemy retreated.

Lovell passed the Hotchkiss to Wren.

'Cover me, Sergeant,' he said. 'I'll check that the tunnel is clear.'

'Right, sir,' Wren said.

Lovell started to walk cautiously forward. Wren put a new strip on the Hotchkiss and crouched in readiness. Then, as he watched Lovell's back, he stiffened. The captain was wearing a pack! Lovell had rushed straight from the tank. Why would he put on a haversack?

Wren started forward again.

'I'm coming with you, sir,' he shouted.

'No. Stay there!' Lovell called.

Wren ran forward. Lovell had disappeared into the darkness. Wren stopped. He heard a single footfall close by, then silence.

'I'm coming with you, sir,' Wren shouted.

No reply.

'I'm coming forward, sir,' Wren called.

Nothing.

Something was wrong. Wren remembered Jacko Bass's words of advice: *If funny things start happening, just remember he's up to something.* Crouching in the darkness, Wren realised with mounting unease that he was silhouetted against the light at the mouth of the tunnel.

Don't trust him, Charlie! Wren threw himself sideways just as a heavy bullet cracked past his head and smacked into a timber support. The sound of the shot followed by Lovell's laughter echoed down the tunnel. A scuffle of running footsteps receded into silence.

'You bastard!' Wren said aloud. Then he added, 'But I know where you're going!'

Wren gripped the Hotchkiss by its barrel and swung it onto his shoulder. He rushed past the tank and out of the tunnel mouth. Outside he turned left and headed up the main street. His sprint carried him through groups of jubilant British infantry who were following after *Dinnaken*, systematically clearing the buildings and cellars on both sides of the street. Most of them were Hampshires and

171

Royal West Kents but there was a sprinkling of New Zealanders who had strayed out of their allocated attack zone. The Kiwis had slung their helmets and were conspicuous in their wide brimmed, 'lemon squeezer' hats.

Wren's headlong rush provoked laughter and derision.

'Where's the fire, Sarge?' and 'Blighty's the *other* way!' were among the many choice comments.

Wren ignored them. At the next bend he found what he was was looking for: the ruins of Flers Church.

Wren stopped and looked about him. Straight ahead, the tank *Dinnaken*, rumbled forward, heading towards the main sqare at the northern end of the village. Crowds of infantry followed on behind, fanning out into the surrounding buildings and alleyways.

He looked to his left; there was no sign of Captain Lovell. Yet Wren was convinced that entering the tunnel was only a blind. From his previous visit in July, Wren remembered the various emergency exits the Germans had dug at intervals along the tunnel. He was sure that Lovell would use one of these at the first opportunity and head for his real objective – Flers Church.

Satisfied that there was no possibility Lovell could have got there before him, Wren mounted the church steps. The building had been shelled to rubble but the shape remained in the stunted ruins of the outer wall and the broken stump of the spire. The door to the crypt had gone but the steps were there. As Wren descended, two Kiwis emerged. Both carried bottles with the necks knocked off. Their fighting-order packs clinked cheerfully. They stopped when they saw Wren; then realised he was not of their mob and goaded him gently.

'Sorry mate,' one of them chirped, 'we've got it all. There's nothing else worth taking – unless you like spuds!'

They brushed past him, breathing fumes and laughing at their good fortune.

Wren continued down the steps. The crypt had changed since his first visit. German engineers had been busy. Electric lights burned brightly, strung on hooks hammered into the outer walls. He could hear a generator chugging away somewhere. Extra supports for the roof were in place and two new exits had been dug, with canvas curtains and steps to ground level. The musty church atmosphere was gone. In its place was a smell of the barrack room and cookhouse: old blankets and boiled cabbage.

One corner had been used as a kitchen. There were various piles of vegetables: potatoes, cabbages and marrows. Among these he found a home-made trench knife. On the floor, beneath a discarded greatcoat, was a German pioneer's bayonet – the one with the saw-topped blade and brass handle. It would have made a respectable souvenir and the Kiwis had missed it. And if he was not mistaken, they had also missed something much bigger.

Wren carefully explored the crypt, learning the layout and getting his bearings. Emergency lighting was provided by oil-filled hurricane lamps hung in strategic places. He spent a good five minutes seeking out and lighting the lamps, then spent a further few minutes making his preparations. Finally, he drew and checked his Luger and located the alcove that housed the petrol generator. After a last look round, he killed the generator. The crypt was plunged into silence and the smoky gloom of the oil lamps.

Wren rested the Hotchkiss machine gun on the generator and settled down to wait. It wasn't long before he heard the sound of footsteps approaching down the steps of the crypt.

22

Back at the tunnel mouth, Hawker was doing his best to set up a defensive position covering the tunnel and the Main Street. In the absence of Lovell and Wren he had to depend heavily on Sergeant Pidgeon.

The sergeant was a tank man through and through. He knew Lovell and Wren had departed on some secret mission but he considered it disgraceful they should leave the tank at such a crucial time. He was glad that Lieutenant Hawker seemed sensible and was willing to take advice. Pidgeon was determined that his tank would do its job to the limit.

They had set *Mavis* in the tunnel mouth so that her port-forward Vickers covered the tunnel and the starboard-forward covered the street. Sergeant Pidgeon considered this inadequate owing to the bend in the road so he had Gunners Green and Black set up a machine-gun on the far side of the street.

Pidgeon was still uneasy and spoke to Hawker again.

'Sir, I don't like this. A tank needs a field of fire. We're vulnerable here. I think we should set up a gun further down the tunnel and get the tank out into the street.'

Hawker agreed immediately.

'All right, Sergeant. You're the expert!'

Sergeant Pidgeon set off down the tunnel with Gunners Large and Small, taking with them a Vickers gun and several boxes of ammunition. Ten minutes later Pidgeon returned and reported that he had set the two gunners up in a good vantage point; he and Hawker prepared to move the tank.

Pidgeon fetched the massive starting handle that had to be fitted to the engine inside the tank. They had just got the crank in place when they heard the Vickers gun down the tunnel start firing.

'Good grief!' Hawker exclaimed. 'The Huns are attacking already!'

'Let's get cracking then, sir,' Pidgeon said.

Togther they began to swing the crank and turn the motor. It was a big job for two men but Pidgeon had great strength and at last the engine fired. Hawker rushed to the throttle, caught it in time and carefully ran it up.

With the noise of the engine neither of them noticed that the Vickers gun down the tunnel had stopped firing; or heard the ominous thud of stick bombs.

With the engine running strongly, Hawker joined Pidgeon at the gear levers to select reverse on both tracks. Just then, the rear hatch was opened from outside and a German soldier thrust in a rifle barrel. He fired at once, hitting Pidgeon in the body. Hawker snatched up his automatic and fired at the doorway but the German had disappeared – only to reappear a moment later and throw in a stick bomb. Sergeant Pidgeon picked up the bomb, tossed it through the doorway and closed the door behind it. The explosion reverberated through the metal hull but the door held.

Pidgeon looked down at his wound; the bullet had scored a deep furrow along his ribs. He laughed wildly.

'Now I know why we've got door handles on both sides, sir,' he said. 'It's so that the Huns can come in!'

He threw open the door again and ducked through, drawing his revolver. Hawker heard pistol shots and went after him.

The tunnel was full of smoke and dust. Gripping his

automatic Hawker blundered forward. He stumbled over dead Germans and then froze as he discerned shapes moving towards him.

'Stand!' Hawker shouted.

'It's me, sir,' Sergeant Pidgeon answered peevishly. He was struggling along holding the wound in his side and supporting Gunner Large who was dragging a wounded leg.

Hawker sprang to help.

'Where's Gunner Small?' he demanded.

'He's had it, sir,' Large replied. 'We had a stoppage on the gun.'

'Let's get back to the tank, sir,' Pidgeon said urgently.

Mavis's engine was still running and they laid Gunner Large on the gearsmen's seat.

'Look, sir,' Pidgeon said intently, 'we can't possibly hold the tunnel now. We'll have to seal it at this end and get out into the street.'

'Seal the tunnel?' Hawker protested. 'But what about Captain Lovell? He might still be in there!'

'Well if he is, sir, the Huns have got him. He's left us to it. We have to do the job as best we can. Let's get out into the street. The Huns will attack down the tunnel again any minute.'

Hawker considered for a moment. He didn't like to destroy the tunnel without orders; it would be an asset once the village was captured. But the sergeant was right: they were being overwhelmed. They couldn't hold out much longer and he had no idea what had happened to Charlie and Captain Lovell.

'All right,' he agreed. 'But how do we seal the tunnel. A six-pounder would do it but we haven't got one. If we drive forward and knock out the nearest supports, we could get trapped under it ourselves.'

'Sir,' Sergeant Pidgeon said patiently. 'We carry a wire

176

hawser on the roof of the tank. We can put it around a couple of the supports and pull them down.'

'Good man!' Hawker said. Together they climbed out of the main hatch and threw the wire rope down in front of the tank. Pidgeon was panting with the effort, his face grey from the pain in his side. 'You'll have to fix the rope, sir,' he said. 'I'll drive.'

Hawker nodded. As Pidgeon went back down the main hatch, Hawker lowered himself from the forward turret and dropped to the ground. As he did so a bullet cracked past his head and sang off *Mavis's* hull. He dragged the rope forward, pulled it around two of the timbers supporting the tunnel and hooked it into a loop. But when he went to the free end it wasn't long enough to reach the towing bracket on the front of the tank.

Hawker called through the open front ports.

'The rope won't reach. You'll have to bring her closer.'

Sergeant Pidgeon cursed and went back to the gear levers. Gunner Large was able to limp about and together they selected first-forward. Pidgeon returned to his seat and began to ease the tank forward. Ahead, Hawker backed down the tunnel waving him on. The tunnel narrowed and closed in around the tank. At last Hawker held up a hand and stooped to attach the rope to the tank. Pidgeon rushed to the gears and helped Large throw them into reverse.

Heavy fire started to come down the tunnel, ricochetting off the roof and smacking into the hull of the tank. Hawker made to retreat but the tank filled the tunnel exit. He was trapped. Hawker crouched in front of the tank and fired his automatic desperately down the tunnel. Enemy fire increased and a stick bomb landed at his feet. Hawker fly-kicked it away and dived head-first under *Mavis's* prow. The bomb exploded off to the side. At last the tank started to move backwards and one of the Vickers guns started to blaze as Gunner Large opened fire from the port sponson. Hawker stayed where he was. Between *Mavis's* tracks and under her prow was the safest place; and he had some protection from the wire rope hanging in front.

The engine roared and the tracks churned at the tunnel floor. The rope became taut and rose from the ground. The timber supports groaned in protest.

'Come on *Mavis!*' Hawker shouted.

Suddenly the supports came away and the tunnel roof came down with a crashing roar. Great chunks of earth and rock fell to the ground and all light was blotted out as dust and debris billowed down the tunnel. Hawker crept even closer under *Mavis's* hull. His only chance was to stay with the tank as it backed out of the tunnel. Dust and earth filled his mouth and nostrils. He coughed and retched in an effort to breathe. He felt himself going and fell to his hands and knees.

Hawker blacked out momentarily but came to as the slack rope was dragged across his body. He grasped it eagerly and hung on. Slowly, irresistibly, the tank dragged him into the light.

23

'Stand! Who goes there?' Charlie Wren's voice boomed hugely around the squat pillars and vaulted ceiling of the crypt. He knelt on one knee in the dark alcove; his right hand held the pistol grip of the Hotchkiss and the long finger of the barrel pointed accusingly at Captain Lovell's heart.

Lovell, caught by surprise, played for time. He peered uncertainly in the poor light, trying to find the source of the voice. He already knew who it was.

'Sergeant Wren?'

He took a step forward.

Wren fired a burst with the Hotchkiss. The noise filled the crypt and bullets whined off the walls and ceiling.

'I said "Stand!"'

'Well, well, Sergeant. What brings *you* here?'

Lovell chuckled softly. His eyes flickered left and right, measuring distances, looking for cover. The big pistol held low in his right hand moved perceptibly to point at the alcove.

'Don't!' Wren warned, and his confidence showed in his voice. 'The pistol; dump it!'

Lovell smiled contemptuously. He let the Fosbery swing from his forefinger by the trigger-guard, then tossed it disdainfully away.

'And the bulldog,' Wren said. 'Use the right hand.'

Lovell fumbled to release the short-barrelled Webley from it's holster beneath his right shoulder. Finally, he drew it and threw it away.

Wren stood up and walked slowly into the light. Lovell, watching resentfully, saw that he carried a Luger pistol in his right hand. His left hand, hanging straight down at his side grasped what looked like a home-made trench knife. He was wearing a German greatcoat secured sloppily with one button. He looked all in.

'Well, Sergeant?' Lovell said. 'What do you want? What are you doing here?'

'Waiting for you.' Wren said mildly. 'I've come because of what happened to Jacko Bass.'

'Private Bass?' Lovell sneered. 'That little tea leaf.'

'Yes,' Wren said. 'As it happens, he was a tea leaf. But he didn't steal the jewels. *You* stole them.'

'What would I want with jewels?' Lovell asked easily. 'My family's never been short of money.'

'It is now,' Wren said. 'You're broke. Your old man gave everything to the PDSA and the Acme Home For Unmarried Fathers.'

Lovell was silent for a moment.

Then he said calmly, 'You've been busy, sergeant.'

Wren nodded.

'I don't like to be had. I needed to know who pinched the jewels. It was too big and too clever for Jacko. You only brought him along because you knew his record and knew you could use him as a scapegoat.'

Lovell smiled.

'I didn't take the jewels,' he said silkily.

'No', said Wren. 'They're still here. You left them over there in the stone coffin when we were here last. Now you've come back for them. That's why you're wearing a haversack.'

'How could I have left them here?' Lovell asked tenta-

180

tively. 'You all saw me take the jewels out of the coffin. Lieutenant Hawker carried them out of the crypt.'

Wren shook his head.

'When we came in here you were carrying a haversack. Inside the haversack were two saddlebags full of tinned food – the same kinds that Jacko was carrying. After you'd showed us the jewels, you dropped your torch. While we were chasing it you threw the saddlebags holding the jewels back into the coffin. In the dark you took the saddlebags full of food out of your haversack and gave them to Mr Hawker to carry out. Later, in the night, you took Jacko out of the tunnel at knife-point and killed him.'

'You seem very sure of this.'

'I am. I've checked the coffin and the jewels are still there. It's the only story that fits.'

'So now you've got your grubby hands on the loot,' Lovell said contemptuously, 'what have you been hanging around for?'

'Waiting for you. I knew that if I was right you'd be back. And I've got a little job to do for Jacko Bass.'

'Which is?' Lovell enquired mildly.

'To kill you,' Wren said.

Lovell shrugged.

'All right. Get on with it.'

Wren shook his head. He turned and walked back to his alcove. Once there, he holstered his pistol and picked something up from the floor. When he returned, his left hand still clutched the trench-knife and in his right was a long, saw-topped bayonet.

'Jacko Bass was a poor, inoffensive little sod,' Wren said. 'He didn't deserve to die like that. Shooting's too good for a bastard like you, Lovell. You fancy yourself with that knife – let's see you use it.'

Lovell shrugged off his haversack and laughed delightedly.

181

'Sergeant, you really are a sportsman.'

He drew the Khyber Knife from its scabbard. Mirror-bright, it gathered the sparse light and leapt from his fist like a flame. Lovell swung it easily before him; slowly at first then faster. The blade sighed its impatience.

Lovell grinned as Wren took a step back.

'You've made a big mistake, Sergeant. This blade has taken nine heads. Five Pathans, three Huns, and of course our mutual friend, Private Bass. Yours will take it into double figures.'

'Don't count on it,' Wren said, circling carefully.

He was thinking that he should have shot Lovell while he had the chance. He thought of the sentry's severed head and the memory almost destroyed him. It was too late now. He would have to stick to his plan.

'Just for the record, Sergeant,' Lovell said easily, 'you're deduction was perfectly correct. When I first hid the jewels in 1914, my only aim was to keep them safe and return them to the their rightful owners. But after the decline in the Blaney finances, I knew that my only course was to purloin the treasure and use it to restore the family's wealth. And if you're wondering how I expect to get away with it, I'll explain.

'*Some* of the jewels will be recovered and returned to Belgium but the majority will be kept in a safe deposit and sold after the war. Disposing of Lieutenant Hawker and the rest of the crew will be a simple matter. On the journey back to base I'll jam the escape hatches from the outside, pour a can of petrol into the main hatch and fire in a signal flare. No one will think twice about a burnt-out tank and a crew roasted to fat. I'll return to headquarters mourning my dead comrades; pathetically clutching the few jewels I've managed to save. Suspicious circumstances? Implausible story?' Lovell laughed softly. 'Believe me, Sergeant, when

182

you're a national hero and peer of the realm, people will believe *anything.*'

'You bastard,' Wren said.

He set down the bayonet, snatched up a lump of fallen masonry and let fly at Lovell's grinning head. It almost worked. The missile caught Lovell off guard and almost got him. He moved just in time and the brick hit the wall behind him, dislodging more debris and starting a small landslide from the roof.

Lovell sprang away nervously.

'You cockney guttersnipe!' he yelled. 'Fight fair, can't you?'

Wren recovered his bayonet.

'You're a low-life, murdering bastard, Lovell,' he shouted, 'and I'm going to finish you once and for all.'

'You fool!' Lovell raged. 'You can't fight *me.* I'm Rupert, Seventh Earl of Blaney. My family fought with Marlborough and Wellington.'

'My family fights with everybody,' Wren retorted.

'You're slum rubbish,' Lovell bellowed, 'the scum of the streets!'

'That's right,' Wren shouted. 'And we eat bastards like you for breakfast. You're mad, Lovell, just like your old man. The barmy Blaneys. This way, your loonyship. I'll put you put of your misery!'

Lovell, goaded into blind rage, rushed forward hacking and stabbing. Sparks flew as Wren parried desperately with the bayonet and fell back.

Lovell calmed himself. He knew he had the superior skill as a swordsman and when the sergeant had chosen to fight with blades he'd made a grievous error. He noted that Wren had not used the weapon in his left hand. The arm seemed stiff. Wren held it forward defensively but always turned and used the bayonet when attacked. Perhaps the left arm was damaged, the result of his pistol shot in the tunnel. Lovell knew he must keep attacking and force Wren to use the left arm.

He darted forward once more, sweeping the knife in an arc across his body. As Wren stepped back, Lovell aimed a forehand chop to the head. Up came Wren's left arm. Lovell turned the blade in mid-stroke. The Khyber Knife flashed down, slicing through Wren's left forearm. The sergeant bellowed in agony and fell back. Something wet and sticky splashed Lovell's face. Part of the stricken limb fell to the floor with the trench knife. Lovell caught an obscene glimpse of white at the stump as Wren's left arm fell uselessly to his side. Lovell roared in triumph and attacked again, driving the near-fainting Wren ever backwards. The sergeant was close to collapse but somehow he managed to keep the bayonet up, desperately blocking while he continued to circle away.

Lovell panted and paused, grinning sadistically at the cowering Wren, eyeing his prey like a cat with a wounded bird.

'Come along, Sergeant,' he goaded. 'It's finished. Why struggle against the pain? Drop the bayonet and offer your neck. You'll feel nothing. Just blissful peace for ever and ever.'

Wren said nothing. He leaned exhaustedly against a pillar, gazing slack-jawed at his tomentor.

Lovell smiled his satisfaction. Everyone underestimated this blade. They couldn't comprehend its sharpness and strength – until it was too late. He sighed pityingly.

'If you continue, sergeant, I'll take the other arm and then the head. Decapitation,' he said conversationally, 'is the quickest death known to man, and the most humane. Most hanged men are throttled to death; they die after minutes of agony. A firing squad will shoot a man to pieces

184

before the *coup de grâce* blows out his brains. In the electric chair – a modern answer to the oldest problem – people are fried to death. In the end you have to come back to the clean blade on the offered neck. Death by beheading is instantaneous – or is it? They say that in France, during the terror, an eminent doctor conducted a study at the guillotine. He asserted that the heads of victims often showed signs of life for moments after being severed. Several were seen to blink. At least one was heard to speak.' Lovell laughed softly. 'What might a severed head say d'you think? Would it be, "*J'accuse!*" or merely: "Ouch!"?'

Outside, a salvo of heavy shells fell close by, causing the walls to tremble and the flames in the storm lanterns to leap madly. Demonic shadows danced across the squat pillars and oily smoke from the lamps writhed like serpents beneath the vaulted ceiling.

Throughout Lovell's tirade, Wren had remained silent. He leaned wearily against his pillar on the verge of collapse. His jaw hung slackly; his eyelids drooped in fatigue. The stricken left arm hung straight down at his side; the right, holding the bayonet, had subsided until the point of the weapon rested on the floor.

Lovell moved lightly forward and aimed a massive blow at Wren's neck. At the last moment, the bayonet came up. There was a clash of steel and Wren stumbled away. Lovell rushed after him, chopping repeatedly, aiming his blows at Wren's head, forcing him to parry again and again. The bayonet drooped lower as the sergeant's strength ebbed and Lovell switched his attack to the right arm.

Wren backed away keeping his sword arm short, conscious that if he extended it too far, Lovell would hack it off. Finally, as he circled, stumbling in retreat, his heels caught some fallen masonry and he fell backwards against one of the stone coffins. Seeing his chance, Lovell rushed in for the kill. He aimed a huge blow to the throat. Wren parried in time but the force knocked the bayonet from his hand and sent it flying.

Lovell cried exultantly, 'Now, sergeant!' but as he raised the knife for the killing stroke he was suddenly, astonishingly, hit in the body by an enormous blow of pain.

It struck beneath his ribs, entered his intestines and twisted upwards towards his heart. The agony was immense, ballooning through his body, swelling the veins in his neck, forcing from his contorted lips and bared teeth a gigantic roar of protest.

'Gaaaaaaahh!'

The Khyber Knife clattered to the floor as his right hand flew to the seat of the pain. There, amid the wetness of his own life-blood, it clamped upon the checkered hilt of a knife and ... *Wren's left hand!* Lovell struggled to comprehend what had happened. The hand and the hilt against his shirt were sticky with something other than blood. There were lumps of some fleshy, fruit-like substance. He grasped some, crushed it in his fist and smelt. And then he understood. It was marrow! The sergeant had stuck a fighting knife into the end of a marrow and held it in the sleeve of his greatcoat. Hence the strange, immobile stance. And when Lovell had hacked at Wren's left arm, all he had cut was the marrow. The splash on his face was marrow juice, the white of the bone was marrow. The rest had been ham acting in a poor light.

Lovell looked down into Wren's sneering, sweat-blackened features.

'It was a trick!' he said reproachfully.

And died.

Charlie Wren held tightly to the handle of Jacko Bass's Shakespear Knife and pushed the body away from him as it slid to the floor.

'Of course it was a trick,' he sighed wearily. 'What do you expect, bloody miracles?'

He wiped the knife on the skirts of his greatcoat, unbuttoned the coat and let it drop to the floor. Then he went over to the little coffin and extracted the two saddlebags of jewels. He put the bags into Lovell's haversack and shrugged the pack on. He collected the Hotchkiss and swung it onto his shoulder. As he crossed to the stairs, he paused and looked at the corpse for the last time. He spoke softly as if acknowledging a promise kept.

'Straight in the guts, Jacko. Just like you said.'

Then he trudged up the stairs into the daylight.

When Wren got back to the tank all fighting had ceased. *Mavis* was parked at the roadside. The tunnel was sealed and no Huns had come down the Main Street – *Dinnaken* had seen to that.

Gunners Green and Black were sitting on the ground eating Maconochie's from the tin. Hawker was seated on an ammunition box drinking tea. At Wren's approach, he looked up in surprise.

'Hello, Charlie. Where on earth have you been?'

'Around, sir,' Wren said.

'Where's Captain Lovell?' Hawker asked.

'I don't know, sir,' Wren replied.

He hadn't yet decided on his story and he wasn't keen to stand over Lovell's corpse answering Hawker's questions.

'We lost Gunner Small,' Hawker said dismally. 'Sergeant Pidgeon and Gunner Large have both gone back wounded. It was all my fault. We should have sealed the tunnel straight away. I just didn't think of it.'

Hawker looked all in. His face and hair were filthy; his eyes red with fatigue. His hands and forearms were grazed and scratched. His tunic was torn in several places and one knee was out of his breeches. Wren had never seen Hawker so low. Even after his own experiences it took him aback. 'We all made mistakes, sir,' he said consolingly. 'Everyone makes mistakes.'

'What's in the haversack, Charlie?' Hawker said. 'It looks heavy.'

'It's the jewels, sir,' Wren replied.

'The jewels?' Hawker said vaguely. Then: 'Oh, the *jewels*! D'you know I'd almost forgotten about them. After all that's happened they don't seem very important.'

'They're *not* important, sir,' Wren said. 'But they're the first thing Sir John Trent will ask about when we see him.'

'Where on earth did you find them?' Hawker asked.

Wren unslung his haversack, extracted the two saddlebags full of jewels and dumped them unceremoniously in Hawker's lap.

'Well, sir,' he replied wearily. 'It's a long story.'

EPILOGUE

Hawker looked at the dashboard watch. It was 9.00 a.m. Below him, two Fokker monoplanes were crossing from left to right. Hawker tapped on the fuselage and pointed. In the front cockpit CharlieWren nodded briefly, cocked both Lewis guns and tightened his lap strap. Hawker knew they were invisible in the morning sun. He thought they had a good chance of getting one, or perhaps both Huns, without being seen. He put the stick over and dived.

It was mid-October 1916. They were back on flying duties and things were going well. Hawker had been right. Once the Royal Flying Corps had adopted fixed, forward-firing guns, they had soon exploded the myth of the Fokker's invincibility. Hard pushed to cover both the Meuse and the Somme, the German Air Service was reduced to patrolling deep within its own lines.

Germany's great ace, Max Immelmann, was dead. The British had since learned that he was the pilot of the Fokker fighter destroyed by Hawker's squadron on 18 June. To Charlie Wren's great disgust, Lieutenant McCubbin and Corporal Waller had both been decorated.

Apart from this, Wren was reasonably happy with his lot. After special duties on the ground, squadron life was a doddle. He had a comfortable billet far behind the lines; the food was good and plentiful; and every evening was his own. Air operations were still dangerous, but with Hawker

189

as pilot Wren reckoned he had a better than average chance of survival.

After returning from Flers, Wren had spoken to Sir John Trent in private. He was determined that Jacko Bass's name would be cleared and Lovell's treachery known – at least to the Secret Service. He had modified his story somewhat, relating how Lovell had fired at him in the tunnel and how he had then tracked him to the crypt, challenged him and killed him in self-defence. At first, Sir John had frowned in disbelief, but as the details of Wren's story unfolded he was unable to fault them. And, as Wren had returned with the jewels, he was in no position to doubt him.

Sir John looked at the full saddlebags lying on his desk and at the tough sergeant sitting across from him.

At last he said, 'Sergeant, I'm afraid we're going to have to keep this story quiet. I'll clear Private Bass's name. He'll be posted as killed in the line of duty. But you must give me your word that you won't tell anyone else what really happened – not even Lieutenant Hawker. Captain Lovell is a hero to the British people. For reasons of morale he must remain one. We'll say that he died at the hands of the enemy, heroically fulfilling his solemn oath.'

'Yes, sir,' Wren said.

It wasn't justice, but it was enough.

Sir John nodded thoughtfully. He regarded Wren in silence, and a shade distastefully.

'So, Sergeant,' he said finally, 'you killed a peer of the realm in hand-to-hand combat. How did it feel?'

'I don't know, sir, ' Wren replied drily. 'He didn't say.'

A week later the following notice had appeared in the obituary columns of the *Blaney Echo*, the *Manchester Guardian* and the London *Times*:

BLANEY, Captain Lord Rupert, VC (post.), Heavy Section, Machine Gun Corps. Late of: Rajputana Rifles; Frontier Force

190

Regiment; Royal Scots Greys. Killed in action 15th September 1916. There is no heir to the title which becomes extinct.

Hawker throttled back behind one of the Fokker fighters, closed to 50 yards and fired. His first burst smashed the cockpit and killed the pilot. The enemy aircraft reared up and dived earthwards.

The other Fokker bolted, turning and diving in an effort to escape. Hawker side-slipped and the FE dropped like a stone. At 200 feet the enemy levelled out fleeing eastwards. Hawker hunted him remorselessly. As they closed on his tail Wren began firing short bursts with the flexible Lewis. He deliberately aimed to the side of his target so that the enemy pilot would turn and swerve, losing vital speed. Hawker held his fire for a close shot with the fixed gun.

At last Hawker fired a long burst. Pieces flew from the enemy machine and the pilot dived straight at the ground. He was well above landing speed but put it down hard. The Fokker cartwheeled and burst into flames.

Hawker pulled up grinning in triumph, but at that moment Wren saw three shadows cross the sun. A glance behind was enough. He gave a pre-arranged signal to Hawker, who gunned the throttle and pulled the stick into his chest.

Wren's vigilance and Hawker's unquestioning reaction saved their lives. The FE rose almost vertically; streams of tracer crackled below and three sleek biplanes flashed past in close formation. Hawker reached the top of his loop and half-rolled off the top. The enemy machines turned to give chase but Hawker was already heading for the British lines.

Wren had turned in his seat and was watching anxiously, but Hawker was grinningly confident. He'd scrapped with Hun biplanes before: two-seater Halberstadts and Aviatiks that were lumbering workhorses. They had forward-firing armament but lacked the FE's agility.

Two close streams of tracer arced past the cockpit. Simultaneously, holes appeared in the port wings and splinters flew from the interplane struts. Wren shouted at him and Hawker kicked it into a tight turn. Hawker held the turn and expected to arrive behind the enemy machines, but with amazing speed and agility the leading Hun stuck to his tail while the wingmen peeled away to circle close by.

Hawker turned tighter than ever, holding the FE in a vertical bank, but the Hun leader effortlessly followed in an identical turn while his two companions began flying wide figure of eights, firing short bursts each time they passed. Hawker looked across the circle at the aircraft turning with him and got the shock of his life. The biplanes were single-seat fighters. They had speed, manoeuvrability and twin, forward-firing machine-guns. The FE was completely outclassed. As if reading his mind, the enemy pilot waved cheerfully to him. Hawker forced a grin and waved back, but he knew they couldn't stay like this all day. He was getting low on fuel. Sooner or later they would have to make a dash for home.

Charlie Wren knew it too. He'd been angered by Hawker's over-confidence, and seeing him exchange waves with the Hun pilot had been the last straw. Labouring against the centrifugal force pinning him to his seat, Wren got the flexible Lewis off its mounting and held it in his lap. He had noted that as the two other Huns turned away on the loop of their 'eight' they were briefly unsighted and facing the wrong way. Wren chose his moment, brought the Lewis to his shoulder and fired a long burst across the circle at the Hun machine. He missed but the enemy pilot flinched at the tracer, lost his concentration and fell into a stall.

Hawker needed no prompting. He kicked the rudder bar, gunned the throttle and dived. They almost made it but the Germans were too fast and caught them just short of the lines. In line abreast and close on their tail the three Huns started shooting in earnest. Hawker jinked and weaved but they had him bracketed. Bullets peppered the wings, slicing wires, splintering spars and struts. Then a burst of fire hit the FE's pusher propeller. It clattered alarmingly and Hawker switched off, shoving the nose down in an effort to keep flying speed. Anti-aircraft fire started to come up and Hawker flung the FE into the thickest of it. Black, stinking bursts erupted all around. Deafening crashes shook the aircraft; shaking their innards; rattling the teeth in their heads. But Hawker's desperate ploy worked. The Huns sheared away, leaving them for dead.

The ground was rushing up. They were still the wrong side of the lines. In a last, hopeless effort, Hawker switched on again. The propeller turned and the engine fired. The nose rose briefly but the crippled propeller beat itself to death and exploded in fragments. The engine screamed in protest and Hawker shut it down. But the brief surge of power had been enough to lift them over the lines. Hawker put it down gently, deliberately knocking the undercarriage off on the rim of a shell hole and letting her settle with a prolonged crash of splintering wood and tearing fabric.

Grinning ruefully, Hawker climbed from the wreck.

'I'm afraid the old bus has had it, Charlie,' he said. 'Did you get a good look at the Huns that attacked us? How would you describe them?'

Wren was busy removing the Lewis guns from their mountings. He thought carefully then turned his full attention on Hawker.

'Single-seat, tractor biplanes. Fast; manoeuvreable; twin Maxims firing through the propeller arc. Typical Hun machines but better than any we've seen before.'

Hawker nodded glumly.

'That tallies with my impression. I'm afraid the machines that clobbered us so effectively were Albatros D-Ones, the new Hun fighter. The French warned us about it a couple of weeks ago but we were hoping they were mistaken.'

'What now then, sir?'

Hawker laughed ironically and kicked at some rubbish from the splintered undercarriage.

'Back to the drawing board, Charlie. I'm afraid the Germans are back in front and we're playing "catch-up". The old Hun has done it again!'

Wren smiled grimly. They had got away with it, but they were beginning to push their luck. He himself had had another narrow escape two weeks ago. After making his report to Sir John Trent on the events at Flers, he'd been given a few days' home leave.

Before boarding the boat at Boulogne, he took his place in the currency exchange queue. He had accumulated 500 francs in poker winnings and wanted to change it into sterling. The man in front of him had a similar amount and was questioned on how he came by it. Having no plausible explanation he was whisked away by the military police. Wren had to think quickly. Gambling in the army was illegal and if he owned up the money would be confiscated.

When he saw Wren's 500 francs, the customs officer pressed a buzzer at his elbow and two burly MPs appeared.

'How did you come by this amount of foreign currency?' the customs man demanded.

'Well, sir,' Wren replied jauntily. 'I'm a barber by trade and in my spare time I do a bit of hair cutting for the lads. I can't charge of course, but they all give me something, even the officers. The major doesn't mind because he likes the squadron to be tidy and even comes to me himself from time to time. I haven't been back to Blighty for a year and there's not many chances to get off the camp. The money's just mounted up.'

Wren's story had a strong element of truth; most of his poker winnings had come from the camp barber.

The customs man grudgingly changed the money into sterling and Wren went on his way. On board ship, he found a WC and stowed the cash in a money belt he wore next to his skin. He'd had a narrow squeak. If he'd been arrested they would have strip-searched him and found the money belt. And in the belt they'd have found the two diamond clips he'd removed from Captain Lovell's saddle-bags before handing them in.

Hawker and Wren collected as much as they could carry from the wrecked aircraft. As they began to make their way back from the lines, they became aware of a frenzied activity everywhere around. Continuous columns of marching men lined each side of the road, choking in the fumes of motor wagons, gun tractors and tanks. Every village, wood and valley harboured gun and howitzer batteries. New narrow-gauge railway tracks had been laid; locomotives and trucks busied back and forth. Multitudes of men, tons of munitions and mountains of supplies moved endlessly forward, as the British army gathered itself for another 'Big Push'.

HISTORICAL NOTE

The Battle of the Somme began on 1 July 1916 and continued until 18 November the same year, when bad weather effectively closed it down. In those five bloody months the British suffered 420,000 casualties, the French 200,000 and the Germans 440,000. Even now, 85 years after, thousands of British tourists visit the battlefield cemeteries every year and ask themselves the same question: Why?

Any attempt to answer must start with the circumstances leading up to the battle. At the end of 1915, Prime Minister Asquith and his cabinet had to face the fact that, after a year of hard fighting, the Allies were no nearer to victory and British casualties already exceeded half a million. They had reluctantly come to accept the truth of Lord Kitchener's forecast on the outbreak of war: that it would last for years and that it would entail a series of bloody battles on the European continent with new, conscript armies containing millions of men.

To liberal, intelligent people this was a dreadful prospect. But when they considered seeking an armistice they had to face the fact that Germany, the aggressor, occupied almost all of Belgium and a large part of France. Clearly, before peace could be considered, this uneven balance of advantages had to be addressed. They must therefore steel themselves for a massive confrontation with the German army – the best trained, best equipped and best led army in the world.

Sir Douglas Haig, Commander-in-Chief, wanted the main British effort to be in Flanders where there were recognisable objectives i.e. recapture of the Channel ports and disruption of German supply lines, especially railway centres. However, General Joffre, the French commander believed a battle of attrition would be necessary (France had already suffered two million casualties) and that the main effort should be made where French and British forces joined – astride the River Somme.

The British Government concurred with the French view and Haig prepared plans for a joint attack with the French in mid-August 1916. However, following the German attack on Verdun, the shortage of French manpower resulted in the offensive being a largely British affair; and the urgent need to divert German resources away from Verdun necessitated bringing the attack forward to early July.

It has been said, with some justification, that the British weren't ready to take on the German army in July 1916. They were crucially deficient in heavy artillery and, although David Lloyd George had greatly improved the supply of munitions, the quality of these still left much to be desired. But for political and strategic reasons: to demonstrate British commitment to the war and relieve German pressure on Verdun, a battle *had* to take place. As Kitchener cautioned: 'We cannot make war as we ought, we can only make war as we can.'

In the event, the high hopes of a breakthrough and a big push forward were thwarted by a combination of constraints: lack of heavy artillery, staff ineptitude, and, not least, the heroic fortitude and ruthless efficiency of the German army. The British also suffered from inexperience and over-confidence. Armies, like children, are naturally fearless at first and seldom learn from the mistakes of others. Kitchener's young army had to learn from its own errors; to discover pain and mortality at first hand. It did so on the Somme.

Even in the later stages of the battle when the new army had learned its lessons, casualties were still horrendous and to our sensibilities unacceptable. The main cause of this was in the nature of the beast. War, like many human activities in the early 20th century, was labour intensive. And given the effect of high explosive on human flesh, heavy casualties were unavoidable. Germany, a warrior state, had the ability to put five million men in the field. Britain and France had no option but to respond in kind or go under.

With regard to this story, although it is based very closely on battlefield fact, it is essentially a work of fiction. The 1st Battalion, Blaney Pals did not exist. They are a representation of all the battalions, drawn mainly from the industrial north of England, that made up the 31st (Pals) Division; that fought and suffered, and many of whose members still lie where they fell, at Serre.

Today the ground around the village is largely unchanged. You can wander in the valley where the Pals assembled, stand on the edge of the copses where they lay waiting and start up the slope towards Serre. It is a melancholy but somehow uplifting experience.

The tanks at Flers wrote their own unique page in history. *Mavis*, of course, wasn't there. She, like her crew, is fiction. In reality, *Daredevil* cleared the Brewery Salient unaided; *Dinnaken* entered Flers alone. *Dolphin, Dolly, Diehard, Dracula, Delphine, Daphne, Delsie, Donnerblitzen* and Lieutenant Sampson's *Delilah* all played their parts. Their victory was clumsy, lumbering, imperfect; but after 15 September 1916 the Western Front was never the same again. To the Allies it was as if a curse had been lifted. The hopeless stagnation of trench warfare had been broken. No longer were infantrymen doomed to attack impregnable positions over impossible ground. At last they could see a way through.

The Battle of the Somme is still discussed in terms of futility and bloody failure; yet there is no doubt that its main objectives were spectacularly achieved. On 24 June when the British barrage began on the Somme, the Germans despatched no more shells to Verdun; and after 1 July 1916 German forces threatening Verdun received no further divisional reinforcements – these were needed on the Somme. To German forces already on the Meuse, it became heartbreakingly clear that four months of suffering and sacrifice had been in vain. This swung the balance of advantage finally and irrevocably in favour of the French. Verdun was saved from capture; and France was saved for the Alliance.

The first day of the Somme was a defeat and a national disaster – almost 20,000 dead; 37,000 wounded. Its effect on the British army and the people at home was immense; and the shock and the human cost is, rightly, still remembered today. But it is also important to remember that the battle went on beyond the first day. 1 July 1916 remains the worst day ever in the history of British arms; but the continuation of the battle over the ensuing weeks and months shook the German army to its foundations. After the Battle of the Somme both Germany and France were in no doubt that a new land power had arrived on the continent of Europe. And it was there to win.